THE POWER

OF THE BIRD

THE POWER

OF THE BIRD

Nenge Series - Book Two

BY

MIKE JELLIFFE

Nenge Books

The Power of the Bird

Nenge Series - Book Two

by Mike Jelliffe

Copyright © Michael A. Jelliffe 2023

All rights reserved

Published by NENGE BOOKS, Australia, Feb.2023
ABN 26809396184
Email: nengebooks1@gmail.com
www.nengebooks.com
Cover illustration by Michael Jelliffe

NENGE BOOKS assists independent authors by publishing quality ebooks and hardcopy books using cost-effective print-on-demand technology. Books published by NENGE BOOKS are availble to buy at www.nengebooks.com

Also available as an ebook: ISBN 978-0-6456758-5-6

ISBN 978-0-6456758-4-9

Dedicated to the people of PNG whose experiences mirror those faced by the characters in this story.

CONTENTS

PREFACE

This book is the second of three in the Nenge Series and continues the story from 'The People of the Bird'. In due time the third in the series, 'The Presence of the Bird', will complete the series. I recommend that readers do read the first book before this one to help understand the full background of the story. It is available as a hardcopy from the publisher at www.nengebooks.com and ebook through regular ebookseller outlets.

Papua New Guinea has been the focus of much of my life since first travelling there in 1971 as a 19 year old, and commencing work there (in aviation, later in church work). I have been privileged to work and live in almost all mainland provinces and have friends in all. Living in remote provincial communities gave me a wonderful appreciation of traditional life and culture, while about ten years in Port Moresby, spread over several decades, gave insights into the many issues faced by urban settlement dwellers. Of course, exposure to politics happens all over the country.

These stories are only possible because of the many insights that I have learned through my PNG friends as they have shared their lives and stories with me. I thank them for that.

The first in this series, 'The People of the Bird', brings the focus on the social, cultural and environmental destruction inherent in exploration and mining ventures, and the possible politics in the shadows. While continuing this theme, this second book in the series shines a light on other social issues, especially those affecting people in lower socio-economic settings, particularly women. These are the kinds of situations that are common all over PNG. However, the story, through the characters, seeks to convey a sense of hope that there can be positive solutions and outcomes in these difficult situations.

People are integrated beings. This includes a spiritual dimension, something PNGians are generally more familiar with than westerners. So woven into the fabric of these stories is a deep spiritual significance which sometimes emerges onto the writing on the page. The validity of a Creator God is acknowledged by Melanesians generally. Most if not all *tok ples* languages have terms for God, though this may include good or evil traits. To what extent is *nenge* God-like?

While seeking to provide incentive for a genuuine recognition of culture as it applies to the practical solutions for the 'earthly' dilemmas of the stories, I have also sought to provide insights into the spiritual dynamics which are recognised in the Bible, and how are these may be played out in what are the kinds of situations many in Papua New Guinea face today. For example, forgiveness replaces payback, love replaces hatred, and compassion replaces judgement.

The response to the first book by both PNGians and others has encouraged me to continue writing the series. I must thank Benedict Kiah for his literay analysis of 'The People of the Bird' which he provided unsolicited. That helped me understand the validity of many aspects of the story to PNG culture and context.

My thanks as always to my patient wife, Kathy, for her continued support for my writing projects in many ways, including proof reading and text suggestions.

Any feedback on these stories is welcomed to nengebooks1@gmail.com.

Michael Jelliffe
Coffs Harbour NSW
February 2023

CHAPTER 1

THE EVACUATION

"A pair of eyes, almost invisible to any onlooker, peered through barely parted blades of kunai grass. A quick scan of the beach, and the eyes slowly descended once again into invisibility in the tall grass. There was fear in those eyes. Their owner, crouched beside two comrades, felt the hair on his neck and arms stand up as adrenalin pumped through his body. He flashed those same eyes at his comrades to pass on a message in silence. There was no sign of intruders, the coast was clear. Still, apprehension was not abandoned altogether."

The storyteller cleared his throat and continued.

"Cautiously the trio crawled forward on all fours through the long grass to where they could get a more complete look at the beach, careful to ensure the sharp edges of kunai did not cut into their bare arms, chest or legs. Three pairs of eyes, wide in their suspense, now scanned the area of concern and together, with a quick glance at each other, agreed there was no danger apparent. At least not that they could see.

"Not a word was spoken.

"Slowly, cautiously, the three crawled through the remaining tufts of dry grass and emerged onto the sand, still keeping a low profile, just in case. Tracks, human footprints, were visible near the water's edge. The tropical ocean on this side of their Pacific island, in the lee of the prevailing wind, lapped the sand with fairy sized waves, barely enough to splash over the youths' toes. The imprints had been made since the last high tide, probably in the secrecy of last night. In silence the three squatted down to examine the prints. They knew they were not of their own. They were of their enemies. And they would return.

"With a growing sense of urgency the three exchanged glances and, as one, sprinted for the safety of the grasslands again. The sooner the chief knew of this development the better. The survival of the clan would depend on the decision they now had to make. Ultimately it would be a decision for life, or death.

"Within half an hour the elders had assembled in the communal area bordered by their village houses. Inquisitive brown faces peered out of the doorways of bare timber houses, which were raised up two metres on posts in case of king tides. Bare-footed children scampered out of the way as parents called to them.

"The chief, an older man with a thinning white beard, gazed at his calloused feet, tapping a small stick on the ground as he listened to the youths. The other members of the tribal eldership looked elsewhere, skyward, at the remnants of last night's fire which simmered in the centre of the meeting area, or at the charcoal-coloured, kunai-grass roofs of the village houses that surrounded them in a circle - anywhere but into the eyes of the storytellers. It was a time to listen and reflect, to draw wisdom from ancient sources of inspiration, not to dwell on the personality of the narrator.

"Finally the chief stood and spoke, not directly to any of the group, yet to all of them.

"'The time has come for us to consider carefully the future of our people, our sons and daughters, and their sons and daughters for many generations ahead,' he said. 'The drought and famine we are now experiencing has the potential to leave us hungry and depleted.' He looked at the ground briefly, tapping his stick once more. 'However a more serious threat has emerged. Our enemies from surrounding islands are stalking us. They too are in the grip of this famine and seeking new ground, with new food sources. They have the ability to decimate us.'

"Several elders raised their eyes and looked squarely into the chief's face. The seriousness of survival was written all over their own as well as his.

"The chief continued. 'We need to quickly assess our options and then take whatever action we agree to. The future of our people, our clan, our language, our culture, is at stake here. Do we want to believe that the Creator wants to abandon us now and cut us off from existence? Do we want to believe that the generations of our ancestors, who fought the elements and their enemies to ensure a future for us, would expect us to now succumb to genocide? Let us approach the Creator for guidance and call on our ancestors for spiritual wisdom and practical help.'

"Slowly, deliberately, each of the gathered elders began to nod in agreement. Then, one by one, sitting cross-legged in a circle round the extinguished fire pit, they began to share their own thoughts, each listening to the others as they spoke in turn. There was no doubt this was a time like they had never encountered before, a time of such crisis that the unthinkable was called for.

"After all had spoken of their concerns about the current situation, the chief spoke once again. On one hand there was nothing to distinguish him from any of the other men in the village or circle of friends now gathered. His hair was greying, and around his shoulders hung a necklace of small shells, supporting a larger mother of pearl shell which adorned his bare chest, just like the others in the circle. But his authority had been distilled in the very cauldron of years of political survival. It was very obvious that respect for him ran deep. His adversaries had long ago abandoned challenges to his authority, and belatedly recognised that his word was life for their community.

"'Let us now talk about our strategy… for survival,' he said, deliberately punctuating the words to express their seriousness. 'We are paddling into uncharted waters. We must imagine the unimaginable, think the unthinkable, plan for the unplanable, and be prepared to risk what we cannot afford to lose. Only then will we find a solution which continues to give life to our clan.'

"Turning his eyes skyward, with his hands extended palms up, the Chief began his simple plea for help from the heavens. Whether he was calling to his ancestors or whether it was the Creator who filled his thoughts and language, it did not matter. In desperation he was calling out for supernatural intervention, the act of desperation only those who know they are trapped can understand.

"The group was silent for many minutes after this prayer. Faces reflected the mental exertion as well as the emotional turmoil each experienced as they struggled to find direction. Some of the women wiped their eyes as tears formed. Others began to discuss it quietly with their neighbour until the hum of their voices filled the meeting area. Some shuffled their crossed legs, others stretched their legs out in front of them, or propped themselves up on their hands outstretched behind them. One or two stood up to stretch before resuming their seat on their woven pandanas leaf mats. Gradually the buzz of voices dwindled until all present were once again attentive to the Chief.

"'I have heard your discussion,' the Chief began, 'and seen the anguish of your hearts as you have wrestled with this crisis and the impact this will have on your families.' He paused, looked down at the bare dirt of the meeting area at his feet once again, beyond the reach of his mat. After what seemed like several minutes, he tapped his stick and looked up again straight into the faces of his elders.

"'I believe I represent your consensus when I say that the only choice we have is to abandon our island and seek new lands for our people. And this we must do immediately.'

"There was no time to waste now. The decision had been made. The footprint-makers could return at any hour, and almost certainly after sunset. The village was gripped with a sense of frenzied urgency.

"The plan to evacuate the island was based around the ocean-going outriggers they used for fishing and travel around the island and out to the reefs which ringed it. Each extended family unit would assemble at their outrigger on the beach that afternoon with as much food and water supplies as they could gather for the journey. The remaining coconuts on the island would be harvested. A small army of young boys streamed out to scamper up the trees and drop the coconuts. Any fishing spears, nets and lines would be taken on board. Taro and tapioca plants would be uprooted and any usable remnants taken. They would employ a scorched earth policy and leave no welcoming traces of food for intruders. They would sail west, aided by the easterly winds which prevailed at this time of the year. There were stories of lands to the west but no one had been there. But this was their only hope.

"By mid-afternoon all had gathered on the beach and together they helped each other drag their sailing vessels down to the water's edge, over the intruders' footprints which were now being erased by the incoming tide, and into the rising tide. Once in the water, the family members boarded their vessels to start their westward journey into the unknown under a light easterly breeze. They would fish on the way and cook on small open fires set on coral covered raised platforms on their outrigger's decking. Clay pots of various sizes, traded from Lapita further to the east, would be used to store food and water, or to cook over the open fire. While they could collect rain water in coconut shells, it could be days between rain showers. Water would be their main challenge and so pandanas leaves would be set up to drain any rain into clay pots.

"These people were experts at sea travel and could read the winds and tides and stars. So maintaining their westerly heading would pose no difficulty, at least until they ran into unfamiliar territory. For the first few days they were able to travel in reasonably close proximity, keeping each other in sight. But by the fourth day some of the outriggers had become separated and the others had lost sight of them. It was difficult to remain in sight at night particularly – navigation lights had not yet been invented, and their fires needed to be shielded from the wind.

Over the next few days the distances between them grew until only two remained close enough to maintain visual contact. They would never know the fate of the others.

"On board one of the boats, the same eyes that had scoured the beach a week earlier scanned the horizon again, still searching, this time for land. Their owner climbed as high as he could up the mast, toes jammed into notches on the mast pole, stripped of its bark.

"'Can you see anything?' called his brother.

"'Just water,' he replied without shifting his gaze.

"The three brothers were craftsman on the seas, experts at guiding their outrigger through calm and choppy waters. Their understanding of navigation by the stars was by now intuitive, having learnt the rudiments of astronomy not from a book but through ancient knowledge passed from father to son for generations. But this trip was extending their knowledge to places beyond the boundaries of the familiar. They were in a real sense entering uncharted waters, as their chief had predicted.

"By the end of the second week they were well and truly into the unknown. They had sailed in deep seas with no reference to land but could sense that something was changing. Was it the smell of land, or the coastal currents? No one really knew, but something was different. Sailors know. They feel it. They knew land was close and decided to tack to the north in the hope of finding it.

"Next morning they awoke to a sight they could never have imagined before. On the horizon, still many miles away, the sun was trying to break out over a massive range of mountains. This land ahead was significant and majestic, awe inspiring, and larger than anything they had ever seen before. Their island home barely rose above the high tide mark.

"It would take another night on the outrigger before they reached land. The majesty of the mountains before them only increased the closer they came. As they approached land they identified the outlet of a river and sailed for it rather than land on the beach, hoping to find a river bank for disembarkation.

"As they continued to scan the coastline, they found themselves somewhere on a beach lined coast which stretched as far as their eyes could see to the north-west and southeast. Flat land with kunai grass and shrubs seemed to dominate the first few miles inland but quickly gave way to forest covered hills and then mountains and steep jungle covered valleys. The river seemed to disappear into the foothills and they quickly lost sight of it.

"Of course their main concern was about any other people. Was this land already inhabited? If so, what were they like? Would their presence be accepted or would they be regarded as trespassers and enemies?

"As they approached the inlet of the river and identified a river bank siding they hoped would enable them to disembark, they continued to scan for signs of inhabitants. It was early afternoon and they saw no sign of fires, whose smoke would be tell-tale evidence of their presence. So far so good.

"The south-easterly breeze up the coast was adequate for them to sail into the river mouth and pull up against the embankment. Setting feet onto dry ground felt good after more than two weeks at sea. Between both outriggers the group consisted of several families including several young men and women and small children. Finding water and food was the first priority, and fortunately, with an outgoing tide, they didn't have to follow upstream too far to find fresh water flowing down the river.

"Setting to work quickly they made up some bush shelters for the night, cutting down sapling trees beside the river bank and tufts of kunai grass which they strapped to beams with plaited grass or thin strips of bark. It would keep them from the sun during the day and hopefully the rain at night until they could build houses of more durable natural resources such as black palm, coconut palm or local hardwoods.

"As the sun set to the west across the expanse of ocean, there was a deep sense of peace that they had reached their promised land. For this they were thankful. The mosquitoes were ferocious and so they huddled round the open fire they'd made. There would be no rain that first night. But they had no inkling of the drama that would unfold before sunrise."

CHAPTER 2

THE AMBUSH

"Pre-dawn in the tropical lowlands bush of Papua New Guinea is a beautiful time. To start with it's the coolest time of the day. It's also quiet, at least until the Birds of Paradise start to sing. Perfect for sleeping.

"Once again the rustle of kunai was the only possible giveaway as eyes peered through the long grass, this time at the sleeping group. The island travellers had indeed been seen well before they set foot on this coastline.

"'I think we've fooled them,' one warrior whispered to his colleague in their language, 'they're sleeping soundly thinking there is no one else here, only mosquitoes!'

"'It was good that we acted quickly to put out our fires before they got close enough to see them,' replied his cousin brother, the black fighting ochre on his face caught momentarily in the pre-dawn moonlight as he grinned. 'They'll wonder now what sort of mosquito has bitten them!'

"Raising his hand so the band of warriors could see it clearly above the grass in the half moonlight, the leader signalled to move in for the kill. Stealth was their weapon, surprise their secret, and generations of head-hunting had honed those skills to perfection. The first the travellers knew was the shrieks and howls that came from the first victims to be speared.

"Fortunately for the brothers the attackers had started their assault on the other side of their camp-site. Filled with adrenalin in milliseconds, they jumped up to face the warriors, fear driving them beyond their human capabilities. But a quick assessment of the situation made it clear they would be the next victims within seconds if they didn't act immediately.

"Pulling up several of their family members, older and younger, by their arms, they knew their only hope was to escape. Seeing a slight break in the warriors lines of attack behind them, the boys and the family members they could push along with them ran with all the strength they could muster, through the gap and straight into the bush. The grass whipped their legs, stinging as the knife-sharp edges sliced like a razor blade through their skin and blood started to ooze down. Branches of trees and shrubs brushed their faces and arms, stinging their eyes and scratching their forearms as they ran into the night. Life was fragile this night, but they were determined not to let go of it.

"Knowing they would be followed and tracked down, they ran for over an hour before stopping to catch their breath and bearings. While there was no sound of pursuers, they knew their opponents were also masters of stealth, and knew their land. As far as bearings go, this was all new landscape but they believed they had travelled inland more or less parallel to the river, so decided to head in the direction they thought would lead them to the river. Fortunately they were correct and within 30 minutes of running, trying to dodge shrubs and trees, found themselves at the side of the river, just as the first rays of dawn gave them enough light to recognise it.

"It was a small delta, wide but shallow; shallow enough to wade in. The water was cool for the sweaty runaways and they plunged into it wholeheartedly, welcoming the relief it gave to their tired and aching bodies. The water stung their cuts and scratches, and turned pink around them as the blood washed from their skin.

"'I think our only chance is to go upriver,' said one of the brothers, 'that way they can't track us over land.'

"'I think you are right,' added another. 'What do you think, Lupiano?'

"The older brother had been surveying the river up and downstream and continued for a minute before agreeing. 'It's upstream we go definitely, we don't want to go back into their hands again.'

"There was no pausing to consider the fate of the rest of their group, but it was certainly on their mind.

"Apart from Lupiano and his two younger brothers, the group consisted of an older aunty, her brother, and three young women and one young boy, all cousins. The aunty and her brother would find the going hardest. For the rest it was an adventure, though one with dire stakes. A wrong move could end with them facing their enemies once again - and certain death.

"So they started their journey up the river. At first they waded, staying close to the river bank, ready to jump into the undergrowth at the first hint of trouble. But as the water deepened and the river became narrower and faster flowing, they were forced back onto dry land more and more.

"At one point when they were forced to go back onto the river bank, the bush grew close to the water's edge. One of the brothers was at the front of the group pushing the leaves and shrubs aside with a stick he'd broken off a tree earlier on. About to step on something coiled on the ground in front of him, he stopped short. It looked like the colour of the ground and leaves, and remained still as he watched it. The others in the group were close behind him and, not noticing that he had stopped, came up behind him in the undergrowth, pushing him forward. With the skill of an acrobat he managed to leap over the object, just as the next person in line, his younger brother, stepped on it. Immediately the brother clutched his foot as the pain set in. The death adder had struck, and the family learnt about snakes the hard way. Little did they know that this land was home to many poisonous snakes, unlike their island home, where snakes existed only in *tumbuna* (ancestral) stories.

"Within one hour the young man was experiencing severe ptosis, the fatal sleepy symptoms of a venomous snake bite. The group had kept walking at first but then slowed to a standstill as the brother's condition deteriorated. They watched helpless as paralysis and pain took him to death's door, and then beyond. With sadness in their hearts they dug a shallow grave and covered him over with stones, now plentiful in the river.

"As night fell their hearts were heavy. Day one in paradise had been like hell. Hungry, exhausted, on the run for their lives in a strange land, and with the loss of many of their number, their spirits were low as they contemplated their future in this nightmare."

"Exhausted in every way, the remnant had slept in fits and starts, woken by every little noise the bush accentuates at night. Thankfully none were of intruders. As first light began to lighten the skies they quickly and silently gathered themselves together, ready to keep moving upstream. A quick wash in the river cooled them down and offered a little refreshment, the water once again stinging their many cuts and scratches, reminding them of the reality of their predicament.

"As the river wound its way into the mountains the group waded in the water where they could, or otherwise forced their way through the jungle which lapped the water's edge. They knew that a jungle track leaves a path for their enemies, the water doesn't. Over the next five days they continued upstream as the mountains became steeper and the river became a series of mountain rapids. Hunger gnawed at their stomachs and made them feel weak. Their energy was being sapped but still they forged on up the river knowing this was their only possibility for survival – to find a place far enough away from the coastal head-hunters.

"Finally they reached a fork in the river and as the shadows of dusk began to close off the valleys, they camped in the area of level ground between the rivers. This gave them a good lookout downstream. Hopefully they could see anyone coming up river well before they reached the fork.

"In the morning, as the sun's rays began to direct shafts of light over the mountains and into the valley, the value of the location became clearer. Not only was it relatively flat, enough for a couple of houses to be built, but it would make good gardening land once it was cleared of jungle. The two rivers gave them two escape routes upstream should the head-hunters return. They would explore both rivers as soon as they could to assess those escape options. But the priority now was to establish some food sources and build shelters.

They would have to learn to cultivate and eat new types of food here in this highlands environment.

"At the same time, Lupiano and his family wanted a sign that this was to be their permanent place of abode. Should they move on further up the river and into the steep sided mountain country which towered before them, or would this place be free from oppressive attacks by the coastal tribes?

"The next day Lupiano gathered the small group together and asked them to join him in seeking the favour of the Creator and the spirits of their forebears here. Hungry, tired and beaten about from their escape from the coast, they knew their physical resources were finished. What other options were there but to reach out to those more powerful than they were themselves?

"'Creator God, benevolent spirits, we cry out to you today,' began Lupiano as the group gathered in a circle in a small area of cleared long grass. 'Hear us we pray, and show us the way forward. Is this where we should put down our roots again, is this to be home for us, or is there somewhere else? Give us a sign to know that we are not abandoned and can gain some hope that we have the favour of the gods from this day onwards.' Their minds flashed back to the disappearance of most of the other outriggers, their relatives and friends killed in the head hunter's attack, and their brother lying poisoned under rocks beside the river.

"'If it is here,' he continued, 'then let us honour you as we seek to understand how to live and eat in this different place. Let it be a place where we can find you and worship you as we see your good hand upon the land. We have nothing to give you, only our deepest desire to find peace for ourselves and our generations to come. This is our prayer.'

"Already Lupiano was stepping up to take on leadership of the small group. No one objected. In fact, everyone in the group had already started to recognise, from the moment he began to pray, that this young man was a natural leader. Time would tell whether he was also a spiritually anointed leader.

"So it was that Lupiano and his family settled beside the Moi River all those years ago," said the storyteller as he concluded his narrative.

"But, dear Lily, the story of their encounter with the bird will have to wait," concluded the storyteller.

CHAPTER 3

THE ARGUMENT

"Why won't you tell me the story of the bird, Justin?" I whined. I'd been pestering Justin for weeks.

"How many times do I have to say it, Lily dear. I can't tell you the story, that's the mistake my grandfather made with your grandfather. Haven't we been over this before?" Justin replied, once again.

"But you promised me you'd tell me and you haven't yet," I said, trying to put pressure on him again.

Within Moiaimba culture, a small Bird of Paradise, known as *nenge* in the local language, had created a mystical aura by revealing itself personally only to those who were to become leaders in the community. But if someone passed on the story of their encounter with *nenge* to someone other than another elder, this second hand account placed the hearer under a curse – that person could never become a leader. This was the curse that Justin's grandfather, a gold prospector in the 1920s, inflicted on my grandfather, Seri. I knew that Justin was not about to repeat this mistake with me, even though the Mambusu community leaders had acknowledged my leadership skills.

"I know I said I'd tell you my story of seeing the bird," said Justin after a minute or two. "But I've had to rethink that. I'm sorry to disappoint you, but I don't want to risk having you fall under the same curse as your grandfather. If *nenge* wants to reveal itself to you, then it will. And when that happens you'll know why I haven't told you myself."

Justin knew I wouldn't like this news, but he was right - it was probably much more important that I was confirmed as a leader by *nenge* and didn't hear the story second hand from anyone else.

Still, I wanted to know the story. Even the elder, Uncle David, stopped short of telling me the bird story when he was telling me the history of our tribe. I looked down and paused before I replied. Justin could tell that I wasn't happy. He couldn't tell that I was only acting to try and get my way though! He'd learn my tricks soon enough when we were married!

"Justin, we've been through so much together in the last few weeks since you came to Mambusu," I said, "and this bird story has been such a big part of it, yet you won't tell me about it. I feel like you're not letting me into your life. That's not a good feeling, especially seeing that we're getting married soon."

I'd tried to use this emotional heart-string argument before. It didn't work then and I could tell it wouldn't work now.

"Lily," Justin replied after a few seconds, "you've got to recognise that this has nothing to do with my feelings for you, and nothing to do with me holding back from you. It has everything to do with me wanting to make sure that you discover *nenge* for yourself. That way your leadership will be recognised in its own right. Otherwise you'll forever be a second hand leader, living on someone else's story."

"So when will I see the bird for myself then?" I shot back at him. Justin was taken back by my directness, but this was something he'd come to recognise and I think respect in me. He'd said before that it's what makes me a great lawyer.

"That's not up to me, it's up to the bird. It'll reveal itself to you when it's ready – and when you are ready," he said, hoping it would be soon, though he'd learned that *nenge* seemed to reveal itself in the midst of extraordinary circumstances. He thought back just a few weeks ago when he'd survived a plane crash taking off from Mambusu airstrip, only to encounter the *nenge* bird in the jungle as he lay waiting with a broken leg for rescuers.

"I hope it's soon then," I echoed, trying to read Justin's thoughts. I wondered what circumstances *nenge* would choose for me?

So much had happened in the last few weeks, it was hard to keep track of everything that had gone on. Justin, an Australian, had come to Mambusu as a government employee, the appointed Mine Warden, to review the coming of a gold mine to the area. But then he'd discovered his roots as a lost child of the Moiaimba through reading his grandfather's diary. The revelation that he was in fact the next headman of the Moiaimba people had been as unexpected as it was surprising. Then came another bombshell by the elders – I was selected to be Justin's wife!

There was something very different about Justin and I saw it the moment he first walked in the door at the Mambusu Guest Haus. He'd driven all day from Port Moresby to spend time here as Mine Warden in preparation for the proposed gold mining operation. He had a confidence and aura about him, like he belonged here. The people seemed to trust him very quickly. And he seemed to fit in at Mambusu so naturally. Like he belonged here.

It wasn't long before I realised I really liked him. It was probably the plane accident that made me realise how much though. When we heard that the plane with him on board had crashed taking off from Mambusu airstrip, I was beside myself and couldn't imagine life without him now. I was so relieved to find him alive early the next morning. He'd dragged himself down to the river, despite a broken ankle, where the search party found him. Of course, I'd gone with them too.

Then came the revelation that he was the grandson of the gold prospector who married my grandmother's sister. She'd died in childbirth and the prospector had taken their little daughter back to Australia. No one had heard any more of either of them until now, when Justin claimed that he was her son, and by birth, the next headman of the Moiaimba – Lupiano.

I'd been waiting for the right time to approach Justin with my idea. His broken ankle was healing well and we'd been going for walks around Mambusu village each afternoon before the rains swept down the valley and consumed the night. He was placing more and more weight on his foot and was nearly ready to dispense with the wooden crutches that had supported him so well over the past few weeks.

We'd been walking for about ten minutes and were well out of earshot of anyone who may have found our conversation of interest.

"I've been thinking…," I started the conversation.

"Uh oh," I heard Justin say, "that sounds dangerous!"

"Well, I think I have an idea," I almost protested, "and I wanted to see what you think."

I paused to give Justin time to concentrate on what I was going to say.

"Ok, go ahead. You do have some very good ideas you know, sometimes anyway," he teased. I loved his cheeky grin.

"I hope this is one too. Why don't we bring your mother up from Sydney to PNG for our wedding? I mean, she has spent her whole life not knowing that she is half Moiaimba. Wouldn't she be excited to come home again?" I said.

Justin's mother, taken from Mambusu by her father, Justin's grandfather, when she was only a few months old, had never known her Moiaimba roots. It seems that grandfather had never told her the story and so she had grown up in Australia in ignorance. It was time to change that.

CHAPTER 4

THE REVELATION

There was another problem I needed to deal with. I'd been in fear of this moment for so long. Now it had arrived. Inescapable. Would I have the courage to face up to it? The courage to declare what could be the end of all I had ever dreamed of? Even the word itself seemed so final, a judgement, a condemnation, which cannot be undone.

"Justin, my dear, there's something I need to tell you," I fumbled. My voice sounded steady but it was a betrayal of my heart.

As the time for our marriage drew closer I knew this was something I could no longer hide from. Nor could I hide it from him. He must know. Or I would be banished to a life of secret shame, forever hiding behind a veil of brokenness, never able to walk beside him in dignity - a dignity which had eluded me so often since that day.

We'd returned from a walk and were sitting in the Mambusu Guest Haus lounge one evening, as we did most evenings, when I finally got the words out.

"I was assaulted at university."

Even as the words tumbled from my lips, the tears began to flow from my eyes. It wasn't the words. It was what seemed like a lifetime of shame, guilt and worthlessness which seemed to spew out with the words.

My hands covered my face. The tears flowed. Now I no longer had a secret. In three words I'd revealed the most intimate details of my life to another person, the physical abuse that had crushed the spirit within me. I longed to be free from it.

But I know that is impossible.

My mind had struggled with this violence as I sought to come to understand its devastating impact on society, never suspecting that one day I would be its next victim. How tragic that so many women have experienced such abuse which devalues them.

Shame enveloped me as I cried, not daring to move my hands and look at Justin. How could he ever wish me as his wife now that he knew? How could I be so foolish and think that revealing my secret could do anything but destroy our relationship?

I'd managed to make sure we were alone this evening in the Mambusu Guest Haus. I'd waited weeks for the chance to tell Justin, fearful of his response yet knowing I must do it or I would not even have a chance to be free. But how would he react? Was I willing to risk losing him to be free?

With head down, I waited. Minutes seemed to be hours. The tears flowed as my heart reached for every hidden negative emotion and flung them out into the open, exposing them to ridicule and rejection. But at least it was releasing them from their place of hiding, allowing light to creep into these places of darkness.

I was sitting beside Justin on the old couch in the lounge room. I waited for him to say something, to tell me it was over, to acknowledge my worthlessness, or perhaps just walk out of the room. I felt the couch move, and then his leg brushed against mine as he moved in close to me.

After what seemed like more hours, I felt his hands against my face as he wrapped his hands around mine and the side of my face. They felt warm and reassuring, without hesitancy. We sat like that for some time, until my tears began to subside and my sobbing faded.

Then, holding my hands in his, he slowly pulled them away from my face and forced me to look at him. I gulped for air in surprise, then shock as I saw his eyes and the tears which now rolled down his cheeks.

As I looked into Justin's eyes, through his tears, I could see a look of anguish. Was he upset because he could no longer accept me? He just held my hands and said nothing.

After a long silence, I could see him trying to say something, as if he knew what he wanted to say but didn't know how to say it. It was the first time I'd seen him lost for words.

"It doesn't matter," he said, quietly yet purposefully, looking straight into my eyes with such compassion that I wondered if I was looking into the eyes of Jesus himself.

"It doesn't change anything…" he paused, "except that it increases my love and respect for you knowing what anguish and heartache you must have been through."

His words were an ON switch for my emotions and the tears began to flow again. Yet these were now tears of joy as an understanding of what Justin had said began to wash over me. Far from rejecting me, he was embracing me, affirming me, forgiving my past, and accepting me as I am. I began to feel a sense of freedom I had never known before. He loved me and accepted me as I was, that's what he said. That was enough for me. I reached out and flung my arms around him as his arms wrapped around me.

Justin waited until we had both stopped crying and our emotions were more grounded.

"Do you want to tell me what happened or would you rather not?" he asked gently.

"I don't know," I replied, "something in me wants to never remember it. But I also want you to know the story so you can understand what happened."

Justin thought about it for a minute or two, and then responded, "If sharing this helps you to be free, then tell me. But if not, it is yours to keep to yourself. I want you to know that you have my heart, and this doesn't affect that in any way. I love you as you are, not as you wish you were."

Once again the ON switch was activated. I was being blown away by the extraordinary love of this man who stood in the face of society to give me value beyond any I could imagine for myself.

"I'd like... I'd like... I'd like you to know..." I said slowly when I'd settled down again, "but I don't want to go over it again, I need to lay it to rest now and move on."

I couldn't think of anything else to say. Justin just listened quietly until he knew I had finished saying what I wanted to say.

"Lily, I'm so sorry to hear of this." Justin responded through his own tears.

"Lily," Justin asked, "you told me before that your parents died in a PMV accident in Moresby. You are a very brave woman and have come through many trials and difficulties and they only make me respect you more."

"Yes, it was a couple of months after this that they died. It was a very difficult time in my life."

Justin was trying to piece together the pieces of my life like a jigsaw that even I had trouble putting together. "Is this assault the reason why you studied family law?" he asked.

"I guess it was," I said, "because I started out thinking I would major in company law but then began to focus on family and personal situations more. I guess deep down I wanted to find a way to get back at these boys who assaulted me, but not only that, find a way to help other girls in the same situation as me. Especially those who are not able to stand up for themselves."

"Do you think that another outcome of your assault is that you have never seriously considered marriage?" asked Justin. His questions were probing and causing me to think deeply about what I had experienced and how it had affected me. But he had hit an emotional raw point.

I thought for a minute. "I just felt that I was never going to be good enough for someone. I didn't think anyone would want me, even though they wouldn't know what happened to me." It was the best I could think of to try and describe how I felt.

I realised that Justin was actually helping me to recognise how this negative experience had affected me, and that was helping me think again about my life.

"I don't understand why you don't feel that way about me too, now that you know?" I said to Justin. His loving response made no sense to me, it was so unexpected yet so freeing.

"Lily dear," said Justin after a pause, "forgiveness is the most powerful force in the world, did you know that? It is far greater than hatred and the desire for revenge or payback. They only take you to a place of bitterness and resentment, and actions you will regret. But forgiveness takes you to a place of freedom."

Justin's words were profound and freeing. He continued. "You've been condemning yourself because someone else took advantage of you. This sin is not yours but someone else's. You were the innocent person. But he needs your forgiveness because that will free you from him as well as free him."

I realised how true his words were. This sin against me had resulted in me taking responsibility for it personally, as if it was my fault. I needed to be free from that. But I was not ready for Justin's next words and they took me by surprise.

"But you need to start by forgiving yourself," he continued, "because you are blaming yourself and that is damaging your self-esteem, the spirit of who you really are. When you regard yourself as unclean and unworthy, you deny the good things in your life, you deny who you really are as a person of value, created in the image of a good God. I see and respect you as a person of great value, and what you have been through only increases my respect for you."

It all seemed so clear now, how I had been my own worst enemy. If Justin could accept me and love me as I am, then I should do the same for myself, and learn to love rather than hate myself.

Justin had more to say so he continued. "The Creator made you as someone precious Lily, someone who reflects the nature of God, someone beautiful in the Creator's sight. But we all have blemishes and things in our lives that we wish hadn't happened. Sometimes it's that someone sins against us, sometimes it is us who commits the sin. But the Creator God demonstrates love to us in a remarkable way, by offering us forgiveness. It is a model of how we should forgive others, as well as ourselves. This is the forgiveness that Jesus offers us."

My emotions were rising once again. I thought I had used up all my tears already, but I was wrong. More flowed. If Justin could forgive and love and accept me like this, it could only be because of what he had experienced himself.

I had been set free. How right I had been when I thought earlier that it was as if I was looking into the eyes of Jesus!

CHAPTER 5

THE MEETING

In the weeks after my confession to Justin, life had been wonderful. I continued to revel in my new freedom knowing that my past would never be a hindrance to my relationship with Justin. Arrangements for our wedding now dominated my time. He though, had been busy following up on the fallout of the proposed gold mine venture and the Nenge Heritage Foundation he had initiated.

There was no doubt about there being gold in the Bright River. Prospectors and exploration companies had several times confirmed the source as being a gold vein several miles upstream from the junction, the immediate area where Justin had recently survived a plane crash and broken his leg.

The formation of the Nenge Heritage Foundation had been a significant initiative by Justin to counter the illegal push by the Member for Moi to exploit the gold for his personal benefit, as well as search for alternatives which allowed the gold to be of benefit to the whole community. Justin was well aware that the Member considered himself as the leader of the Moiaimba people, and that he should expect some under-hand tricks from the Member as he, Justin, rightly claimed his headman status as Lupiano.

I was appointed as legal officer of the Foundation and frankly it was thrilling to be able to see us starting to make progress with a future for my Moiaimba people. Justin, as Chairman, called another meeting of the Foundation committee now that he was no longer impaired by his leg and could move about freely again.

"Lady and Gentlemen, it's so good to be back again and to be able to focus on what is important to us now," he said as he addressed the meeting. "We are in a battle. We cannot allow the shine of gold to dazzle our senses, like our Member seems to have done. The plans we make will need to be in the interests of the community, not ourselves. They need to keep in mind that what we do now will impact our children, grandchildren and generations to come."

The committee members were all tuned in to hear his every word, glad that he was back on duty again.

"Why don't we start by giving each of you a chance to review what you may have been able to do in the last six weeks. Lily, can you be the first?" Justin asked me.

During the time we were in Port Moresby during Justin's initial medical retrieval from the crash and his treatment and recovery, I had taken the opportunity to visit a number of offices and collect information. These gave me a diverse range of facts and figures, information from tourism to mining, biodiversity of fauna and flora to the legalities of exploration and mining leases. I was most interested to see what ideas there were to have alternatives to just having the gold mined by a multi-national corporation at the expense of the community. So as well as looking at options for alluvial mining for which we could obtain a lease and therefore maintain control, we wanted to consider eco-friendly tourism opportunities. These would showcase the amazing beauty of the valley as well as possibly allowing small scale gold extraction as a component.

So I gave a very brief summary of the places I had visited and the information I'd collected. There were no conclusions yet, just a bunch of ideas and supporting opportunities. The group was keen to hear of these and several asked questions of me.

Justin then went around the group and each contributed comments.

Hendros Kipa, who was a local trade store owner and now also Treasurer of the Foundation, advised that he had been able to prepare to open a bank account and was therefore ready to receive and deposit the funds promised by Justin which would form the initial donation to kick start the Foundation. He just needed committee signatories on the bank paperwork.

Justin had, at the groups' first meeting, before his accident, advised that he was donating his "going finish" pay to the cause. This was a sizeable sum after many years as a senior public servant in PNG, and came to around 800,000 kina once he had taken out what he needed for his own costs to build a house for us in Mambusu village. The impact of his willingness to invest everything back into his new community had taken us all by surprise but set the tone for us as we also considered our own individual contributions, whether in funds or time and effort, what Justin called "sweat equity".

Umbare David, also a senior village leader and former Teacher, now Community Liaison Officer for the Foundation, reported that the Member had been lying low and there was nothing much to report on his movements except that he was awaiting the outcome of a Leadership Tribunal hearing. We agreed to all continue finding out more in our respective portfolios and to meet weekly from this point of time on.

The other members of the Foundation committee were John Aitomo, local Council President and in charge of local government liaison for the Foundation; Paul Wondanga, head teacher of the local primary school and now company secretary; and of course, myself as legal advisor. Oh, also Kila Woro, who lives in Port Moresby. Kila was Secretary to the government department that Justin previously worked for and they became good friends. Kila was appointed as national Government Liaison Officer for the Foundation.

Paul kept a close ear to the ground when it came to politics, and his turn to speak was last.

"I think the Member's relationship with the South East Asian consortium is dead in the water," he stated, "so I have no idea what the Member may do now. However we know that he will still try and work behind our backs to pull off something which benefits himself. We need to be very careful about our movements because he will have his spies around the community watching us. So we must keep our meetings secret from the public and be careful what we say."

The other committee members nodded in agreement.

"Oh, one more thing," he suddenly added, "I heard that the government may be calling an early election soon."

At first we all just nodded as we listened, but his last sentence suddenly changed that! An election would mean a true political battle - and everyone knows that politics is a dirty game!

I looked at Justin and saw the dilemma he now faced. Should he stand for election as Lupiano, the traditional leader of the Moi people? Would he be up against Lupo Warina, the current member? Was his leadership role best served by becoming the political leader representing the Moiaimba people in parliament? I saw the look of confusion in his eyes as he started to realise that the future had now changed.

CHAPTER 6

THE DATE

A few days after suggesting we bring Justin's mother up to PNG to visit, I thought he was ready to talk more about it. I knew that he'd need time to really think it through so I didn't rush him.

"So, when should we bring your mother up to visit? Don't you think our wedding would be a fantastic opportunity?" I asked him one evening.

"Yes, I really do like your idea Lily. But she is well over 70 years old now so we'd have to be careful not to overwhelm her. And while she is in pretty good condition health wise, she is still over 70 and her health is not like a 30 year old," replied Justin, casting his eye towards me as he mentioned 30! I turned my head slightly aside to hide my smile from his reference to my supposed youthfulness at 31!

"I've told her that I've met a wonderful girl who I am going to marry," he said, "but I'm not sure how to tell her the rest of the story, you know, about her PNG heritage. I'd hate to give her a heart attack if it was a total surprise!! I haven't even told her about grandfather's diary." It was in reading the diary recently that Justin had discovered his own PNG heritage and his mother's story.

"Well, there's only one way to find out, isn't there," I replied. Either he told her the story or he didn't, but there was no way she could visit us unless she knew the full story. It would be a homecoming for her in every sense of the word.

"How about we do this," Justin suggested. "We'll invite her to come up for our wedding. I know she'll love that. But I'll need to accompany her for the trip up from Sydney, so I'll give her the story when I go down to get her. I'll make sure we have a few days for her to process this before we come."

"That sounds great," I said. I think Justin picked up by my tone of voice that there was something else on my mind now. He looked at me, as if to say, 'and….'

"And…" I said after turning to look him straight in the eyes, "when are we going to set the date for our wedding? I feel like you've been delaying making a decision on it and I don't know why." There I go again, being so direct!

Justin paused. "You're right," he said confidently. "Absolutely right. I've allowed other things on my mind, especially the Foundation development and the upcoming election, to distract me from thinking too much about our wedding. But yes, Lily dear, we need to make a date now and then you have some certainty about the future."

What about his certainty too, don't we both need it? I didn't say anything this time. At least I had his agreement on making a date.

So as we sat together in the Mambusu Guest Haus lounge room, we pulled out a calendar and began to plan.

"I think it should be before the elections because if you are elected, then you'll be too busy in the new role and we can start that as a married couple," I said.

"I think it should be after the election because of all the time I'll need to be away and out in the electorate campaigning for the election," he said.

"If we wait too long then your mother's health could deteriorate and she could even die, she is over 70 after all, and then she would never visit," I countered.

"It will take time for mother to get a passport and get ready to come so we cannot rush it," Justin replied.

"We can live in the Mambusu Guest Haus until our own house is built," I said.

"I think we should wait until our own house is built so we can move straight in and start our married life in our own home," he said.

"But the elders have made it clear that the community has marked us to be married so they will not want us to wait forever," I argued, my voice getting louder.

"But we do need to have time to really get to know each other well before we actually get married and are living together," Justin replied.

We were now staring at each other and we could both feel the tension growing! This man was so frustrating! Why could we not find any point of agreement on this, our wedding date! How on earth could we hope to live together as married couple if we couldn't even agree on this!

The knock on the front door of the Guest Haus startled us. I jumped off my chair to open the door, glad to be distracted, wondering who would be coming here in the evening like this. It had started raining soon after we started talking but we'd never even noticed the sound of rain on the roof or dripping in the downpipes.

"Come in quickly," I urged the visitor as he lowered his umbrella, spilling water drops onto the verandah.

"Sorry to disturb you this evening, I'm sure you were having a lovely time together," said Umbare David. Justin and I looked at each other. He was the first to start laughing, and it was infectious. I too began to laugh.

"Oh Uncle David, I'm so sorry to laugh," I said, "we'd been having a rather serious discussion actually." He smiled as we continued laughing.

"I won't be long but I have something I need to talk with you about," said David. "The elders and I have been discussing your marriage."

Our laughing stopped suddenly and Justin and I looked at each other, somewhat bewildered. How did he know what we were talking about? What had the elders been discussing?

When David had our attention again, he continued.

"Yes, we've had some thoughts about your wedding date. We have some traditions in our culture in relation to the time frame. As you will know Lily, before a man is married in our culture, he must undergo certain rituals. These take time. Initially the tribe will determine that the woman selected is suitable in personality and character for the man. Then the man must undergo some initiation to ensure that he has passed into manhood and is fit to be a husband. This usually involves up to six months living in the bush and putting his skills as a hunter to the test, finding his own food. He must survive by himself in the bush, and is sent out of the village naked and only with a bow and arrow. If he cannot survive the required time and returns to the village early, usually starving hungry but hopefully no longer naked, he may not be considered a suitable candidate to marry the girl."

David looked up at us with serious eyes though I could see he was quietly amused at his last comment. He could also sense that we were already starting to feel a little uneasy about what he was saying. I knew what these cultural expectations were but Justin didn't and I could see the look of horror on his face. Were the elders now making further claims to what he must do to marry me?

David continued, "During this time the man is not allowed to see the girl at all."

I heard Justin swallow, in fact gulp. The reality of not seeing each other for six months was unthinkable. We would not be able to handle that, I know.

"The period of betrothal finalises in a week of ceremony and all night *singsing* dancing," said David, finishing his summary. "Justin, you showed great interest in our customs when you first visited us all those years ago when you came with the high school rugby team, and have continued to do so. Now as Lupiano we want to help you to continue to learn our customs and truly be a Moiaimba man rather than someone looking in from the outside."

Justin was now deep in thought, wondering what all this now meant. Six months alone naked in the bush with just a bow and arrow? That thought alone was unthinkable! Is David saying that Justin could now no longer marry me unless he goes through these cultural initiations?

David stared at Justin, a serious look on his face, giving Justin time to take in all that he had said. He seemed to be savouring the moment in seeing Justin under pressure. The tension in the room had risen again.

Suddenly David burst into laughter, slapping himself on his leg, hardly able to contain himself on his chair. Now it was his turn to joke. We watched him, not knowing whether to laugh ourselves or not, but gradually we started to recognise his joke. After a few minutes he spoke again.

"Oh Justin, we've decided that just as we allowed your grandfather to skip most of the cultural expectations when he married Leelak, we have decided to allow you to do the same. You don't have to go naked into the bush for six months!" David burst into laughter once again at the thought of it, and Justin and I cautiously joined in. "We will have a few days of *singsing* and celebrate in our traditional ways but we won't put extra demands on you both."

The look of relief on Justin's face was like a new groom who finally sees his bride coming down the aisle! He was so thankful and began to appreciate more the prank that David had pulled on him! He too began to laugh, and the three of us enjoyed a few minutes of hilarity.

"I actually did have some good news for you both," continued David. "We believe that it's in the best interests of the community, especially if you are considering standing for politics, for you to get married sooner rather than later. Given that the elections are probably in less than three months time, we would like to see you married well before that. Our strong suggestion is that you schedule the date for about two months from today."

I couldn't believe his words! The community leaders must have been aware of our predicament and had made the decision for us, one I was very happy with! I looked at Justin wondering if he was happy with this intervention. He was smiling from ear to ear.

CHAPTER 7

PRIME MINISTER

Lupo Warina's walk was deliberate and purposeful as he wound his way along the corridors of Parliament Haus in Waigani. A smile spread across his face, though there was no one else in the corridor to witness it. His office in the Round Haus, to the back of the main building, where Ministers and Members were allocated rooms, was, until later today, further down the hall than those more senior to him.

But he was happy. Very happy. Election time is always good for the winners, and he was a winner. His campaign had gone beautifully, though he didn't care to recall how many 10 kina notes he had distributed, flowing out of his pocket like an ATM machine for anyone who pressed the right buttons. But succeed he had.

His thoughts turned to the welcome he was about to receive when he entered the parliament in a few minutes. His eyes glimpsed at some of the paintings and photographs that lined the natural wood covered corridor walls. Soon he would enter the Chamber and be witnessed not only by the masked spirit faces which stared down from their hangings on the magnificent rosewood wall panelling, but by his new parliamentary colleagues.

What a roar of welcome that will be! The new Prime Minister! Lupo revelled in the praise and adoration which was about to be heaped on him, and lifted his chin a few millimetres higher in anticipation. His heart started to beat a little faster with every step closer to the Chamber door.

A security escort stood at the door watching the new Prime Minister as he approached. Just as Lupo reached the door, the guard opened it to allow Lupo to stride in without any hesitation. The noise started as soon as the parliamentarians saw him enter, and in no time it seemed that every member of the house was adding in their contribution to the cacophony. The noise was almost unbearably loud but Lupo began to hear some individuals calls through the mass.

"Rabisman, lusim mipela!"

"Yu giamon!"

"Go bek long ples!"

"Stilman, nogat ples long hia!"

CHAPTER 8

THE NIGHTMARE

The mountain areas of Papua New Guinea are majestic and beautiful. Especially on mornings like this. At dawn the sun rises over towering peaks, illuminating the dark shadows of the night as its fingers creep deep into steep sided valleys. Tree by tree the incognito of darkness is exposed, its hidden shadows revealed. Mist begins to seep up from the jungle, weaving a mystical pattern, invisible to touch but clouding out visibility.

Soon the scenery is cocooned so that no other world exists except that within a few metres of where you are. Eventually, as the rising sun begins to beat down on the fog, heating it up, spots of sunlight begin to emerge through it. Patches of blue sky fight their way through the evaporating white blanket. Simultaneously this sea of white begins to lift, as inconspicuously as it came. The tops of the closest trees become visible, then the nearest foothills, until by mid-morning the fog has transformed into fluffy white balls of cumulus cotton wool floating in the sky.

Whatever the majesty of the mountain mist may have been on this foggy morning, it failed to impress the Honourable Lupo Warina MP. Startled when he woke suddenly from a dream gone bad, he was dishevelled and annoyed. While his house in Deria village commanded the most exquisite of mountain views looking out over the fog-encased valley, his mind was on other things. Sitting on a log outside his family's kunai-grass roofed village house, he recalled again with distaste the events of past weeks.

As the Member for Moi electorate, which was home to the Moiaimba people, he had been humiliated beyond reason. His attempts to introduce a mining venture had been scuttled. A year of working to get Namel Mining Pty Ltd, a South East Asian consortium, an opportunity to establish a gold mine in the area had been thwarted. And in the process he'd been humiliated by the courts. Here he was, back in his village, waiting for judgement to be passed following his referral to the Leadership Tribunal. A month ago he had everything going in his favour. Now he had nothing, not even his dignity as leader of his people.

Lupo's mind began to unravel the events of the last few weeks to try and figure out exactly where things had gone wrong. He'd planned so carefully, been so confident that his scheme would work. It'd come as a complete shock when in the midst of a challenge to the validity of an agreement to purchase land for the mine, the judge had heard other complaints against him.

No one else had seen the potential of the gold that flowed so freely down the Bright River and through the junction to become the mighty Moi River. Except him. He was the one who had the vision of a gold mine. He was the one who had made the contacts and convinced the consortium that it was worthwhile. He was the one who helped establish Namel Mining Pty Ltd. He was the one who negotiated to establish the Namel Community Trust fund to receive 15% dividends for the benefit of his people. He was the one appointed as Trust Chairman by Namel Mining. And he was the one who established Moi Futures Pty Ltd as an outlet for disbursement of funds from the trust fund.

It was Moi Futures that had been the problem for the judge, and, as it turned out, also for the Namel Mining company. Honourable Warina was found guilty of fraud. Everyone knows you have to have a fund which greases the system, oils the cogs and makes things work properly, and that's what Moi Futures was – a fund to make sure things went ahead. Lupo rejected the language used by others in the court room, where words like "slush fund" and "nepotism" were overheard.

Kila Woro, the government Department Secretary.

Yes, he was partly responsible. Lupo had entered into an arrangement with him to help smooth things for Namel Mining. He'd given Kila 10,000 kina towards his retirement house costs, and two pigs for his son's bride price. The fact that he'd used a Moi Futures cheque to pay for these was regarded by the judge as fraudulent.

Namel Mining had also claimed that he'd commenced Moi Futures as a subsidiary of Namel Community Trust, with himself as Chairman, without their knowledge or approval. But these Asians know that you can only get projects going when there is enough money to grease the wheels. So why were they suddenly surprised to discover that he was doing just that?

Lily, the lawyer.

She's got to take some of the blame. The girl from rival

Mambusu village. The sometime receptionist at the Mambusu Guest Haus with a law degree. Thought she was so smart to humiliate him in court.

But then to cut him off at the knees outside the court was unforgivable. The arrogant look on her face as she announced that there was a new headman for the Moiaimba people. That's ridiculous, how could Lupiano suddenly appear out of nowhere? And now she was going to marry him!

Lupo Warina's mind wandered once again over the story embedded into Moiaimba cultural history. A gold prospector had made friends with the local community at Mambusu and married one of their finest young woman, the headman's daughter. She'd died in childbirth, leaving an infant daughter whom the gold prospector had taken with him back to Australia. That was the last contact either the gold prospector or his daughter ever had with the Moiaimba people, way back in 1923 or 1924.

The story was legendary. But its significance lay in the fact that if the child born to the headman's daughter was a boy, he would be the next headman. However, if the child was a girl, then it would be her son who was the next headman, Lupiano. So the story could only be true if the child who was taken away from them at just a few months old actually had a son. And if that son had now returned, over seventy years later.

Could that really be possible?

There was one catch though. The gold prospector had carved a beautiful rosewood chair while waiting for the birth of his child. He took that with him as well but made a promise to the people. A promise that has lingered in the shadows of Moiaimba history ever since. He said that the person who returns with the chair would be the next Lupiano.

Lupo reflected on this for a long while. If, as Lily had claimed, there was a new Lupiano, then the proof of that would be in the chair. If he didn't have the chair, then he would be an imposter. But if he did have the chair…. Lupo realized that his own claim to be the true leader of the Moiaimba would be rightfully challenged.

Justin Lupiano Orlando.

Yes, he's the one who has now claimed the position of Lupiano. He is the one Lily said was 'The One'. This Johnny come lately from Australia had been at the heart of Lupo's humiliation. The humiliation of being disrespected as the true leader of the Moiaimba people - and dethroned by the words of a woman.

Lupo Warina MP had no doubt that his real battle was with Justin Orlando, the one who now claimed to be Lupiano, the son of the headman's daughter.

'We'll see who wins,' he thought to himself as he started to review again the schemes now being cultivated in his mind.

CHAPTER 9

THE SETTLEMENT

During his frequent trips to Port Moresby on official business as a Member of Parliament, Lupo Warina would often take the opportunity to develop his further interests, or, as the case may be, develop his interests' further. These were generally opportunities that also added interest to his assets in one way or another. Cash was preferred of course, but next to that was land, which could produce cash.

He remembered a recent visit to the growing Nine Mile settlement outside Port Moresby, when he was feeling excited about the prospects ahead. As he picked his way along a muddy path in the settlement, he could see the potential a land grab could have.

In the early colonial days, only a handful of Papua New Guineans, natives, as they were referred to then, were allowed into the small towns that were forming around the country. They were engaged as labourers and were not permitted to stay in the 'colonial - whites only' towns beyond their daytime work responsibilities. In the years leading up to self-government (1973) and Independence (1975), more and more freedoms were being introduced which allowed Papua New Guineans to dwell in the towns.

Initially it was restricted to those who were needed for employment, such as cooks and domestic workers, who were allowed to live in houses usually at the back of the properties of their colonial masters. Then families were permitted to join them, and the emergence of a new generation of urbanites began, second generation children whose home was in the town. Then the door began to swing open for relatives and extended families to visit and remain. All now needed a place to live and call home, and so the formation of squatter settlements on unused portions of land began to sweep the towns.

From the late 1960s there was a boom in urban migration which saw an urban growth rate of over 18%. The National Statistical Office recorded urban growth rates of over 5% for Port Moresby in the 1980s and into the 1990s. In the 15 years between 1966 and 1980, the city tripled its population of around 40,000, reaching almost five times that by 1990.[1] The reality may have been more than that because of the constant itinerant migration that was occurring, as people visited their relatives for a few months and then returned back to their village.

As family groups entertained new arrivals from their villages, *tok ples* communities began to spring up, mono-cultural communities of settlers who began to express their own culture within the confines of the settlements. The branding of these communities in identification with their cultural roots began to extend to the naming of the settlement based on the dominant tribe or language, or town of origin.

Thus it was that a growing group of settlers originating from the Moi electorate had begun to call their corner of Nine Mile settlement their home. To others, it was referred to as "Mambusu" settlement. Nearly everyone in the Moi area had some sort of relative living in Mambusu settlement. In fact, this community had become more of a political people power base than the village community.

In the years since the last election, Lupo had been quietly watching the growth of this new settlement community on the edge of Nine Mile for two reasons. First of all was the potential to invest and make a profit from the interest in real estate there. Secondly, he realised that this was where his chances of re-election would 'make or break' - if he could win the votes of the settlers, he was guaranteed to win his seat. He would need to make sure Justin Orlando remained in the dark about this settlement.

He lurched to one side and reached out to balance himself against the grubby fibro wall of a half completed shanty house as his foot submerged into a watery, muddy puddle. There were no services in the settlement. Water runoff, whether from people or rain, created a constant trickle of sloppy drains meandering between, and sometimes under, the houses. These flooded during rain, further distributing the wastage with it. Half completed houses were everywhere, no doubt in large part due to the inability of the owners to afford the materials needed to complete them. Many had sheets of plastic or blue tarpaulin tacked up to try and keep out the rain or sun.

On this day he was keen to inspect the settlement area and become more familiar with its layout, especially what potential there was for land development. But as he walked around the settlement and greeted his tribesmen, he was also building the relationships that would be necessary to win their votes. He was ready with promises for improvement and development and had pocketed a few 5 kina notes just in case anyone needed a small helping hand. Some would have been happier if he brought roofing iron and nails with him, and several requests for this were subsequently received.

Lupo was well aware of some of the challenges in land development around Port Moresby. Land that was not already declared as crown land, having been purchased for the administration regime with a mirror and axe many years earlier, was customary land, owned by the local historical clans in the area. This created the challenge - how do you sell land which is not yours, but belongs to either the crown or the local landowners? Lupo had discovered the answer as he'd watched other colleagues in high places tackle this same question. The answer - get in first and ask questions later! Give the settlers a sense of security over their plot by selling it to them. Once the money is in your hands, there is very little people can do when the real landowner comes to challenge the sale.

Lupo had engaged some surveyors to draw up lots of the suburb, allocating a fair price for each lot, which would come with a fake title, issued by him but meaningless in the eyes of the Lands Department. He kept the planning diagram in his mind as he walked around the settlement, mentally taking note of the best locations for developing facilities which would enhance community life.

Back at Waigani after his tour of the settlement, Lupo took off his shoes and rinsed off the muddy residue which had worked its way into the inside of the shoes. He'd arranged to meet up with some fellow entrepreneurs, all members of parliament with him, to discuss the project and ensure every success was guaranteed. The others also had their own *tok ples* settlement communities in the same area and so a combined project would look more reassuring.

"Bro, how did your visit to Nine Mile go?" asked one colleague as they got together in his office.

"I can't believe how much potential there is for us," replied Lupo, now trying to fit his socks back on. "I mean my people are very keen to get some help, the place sinks with stagnant water in drains everywhere, it can't be hygienic. The sooner we can get the place cleaned up, the better."

"Bro, the rest of us have been thinking about this," the other colleague said, seeming like he was now the spokesman for the group. "We reckon that there is a better way for us on this project."

Lupo looked up, forgetting about one sock half on his foot.

"Yeah," said another, "the people there can't afford anything, so how do we expect them to buy their lot when it's developed? So we reckon we need to move them off the land so we can do a proper development and then sell lots to those who can afford it."

Lupo was caught a little off guard with this development and the others could tell by the look of surprise on his face.

"You mean we evict the settlers?" he asked.

"That's right, we kick them off so we can develop the land properly and create a proper housing project there. We can easily justify that by telling them that they will be eligible to receiving housing when it's done."

"But many of those people have lived there for years, it's their home isn't it? Where do they go if we evict them?"

"Listen Bro," said the first colleague, "you yourself just said the settlement is an unhealthy mess. The only way to clean it up is to get rid of the people and their temporary houses, get the bulldozers in, and then start again and build proper permanent houses, along with the other infrastructure needed."

Lupo could see that things were changing. The idea of developing the settlement for the benefit of the settlers had now turned into evicting them and starting again. He could see that his people, among the poorest, would have little opportunity to afford new housing. He was being bull-dozed into a new plan, and he was very uncomfortable with it. If this became known among the settlement residents, he would lose his support base quickly.

"I don't like the sound of this," he ventured to say, "because my constituents think I am doing things to help them."

The second colleague quickly interjected. "Hey, Bro, you don't need to worry. For Moresby to develop, we, the leaders, need to take steps to control this unchecked settlement growth, and developing new housing estates is the best way to go. If you want the best for your people, then you need to get on board with us on this. Otherwise you'll be left out, and Mambusu settlement will become like a giant, mud-filled pothole in the middle of a highway."

"So what do I tell the people?"

"Only what you've already been telling them - we want them to buy into development of their settlement."

Lupo realised he had little option but to go along with the others. He would have to be careful about what he said publicly. He needed their votes, and by the time any evictions started, the elections would be over, so maybe it won't be too bad, he thought. Still, what little sense of morality he had was being challenged.

"OK," he said to the group after thinking it over for a few minutes, "I'm in."

There was still one thing he would need to be able to join the syndicate. Money. And the best way to get money was by getting gold. His thoughts turned once again to the gold seam on the Bright River near Mambusu. The quickest way would be to get an alluvial licence and get the gold from the river that way. He needed to get back there and re-survey for a fresh application for an alluvial licence.

CHAPTER 10

THE SHED

The Honourable Lupo Warina MP was in many ways an entrepreneur. He was always on the lookout for more opportunities to develop enterprises which might help his cause, which was, of course, to enlarge his own empire. He had already demonstrated that, in his estimation, ethics and morality were flexible. The end result may justify the means even if both were suspect.

So it's no surprise that he found opportunities within the small community of Mambusu to develop enterprises which, shall we say, provided a substantial return on his investment. In this particular case, his investment was a tin shack on the edge of the town on land owned by a distant relative. The shack, made of rusting, corrugated iron sheets nailed to a frame of natural timber poles, some still coated with bark, provided a safe place for patrons to meet out of sight of the rest of the community - especially their wives. The other investment involved was a constant supply of playing cards, and some stocks of beer, driven in from Port Moresby also out of sight, usually at night and under a tarpaulin covered truck. It was not unheard of though for the beer to taste more like 'home brew' when actual beer stocks became low!

Unemployment was high in Mambusu and so the opportunity for men to get together and socialise was recognised as a valid need in the community. This was exactly how the Member would justify his illegal gambling house if anyone questioned him about it, but hardly anyone did. What good would it do to disturb the status quo established by the most powerful man in the community? Generally though, he tried to keep himself at arm's length, so it looked like it was his relative's business, not his.

The gambling house was commonly referred to as the 'Ace Place' by patrons, which became corrupted to *'As Ples'* in Tok Pisin, with its double meaning of being at home, and perhaps at the tail end of society. The Member relished this sense that the men who visited would feel that this *'hausman'* was more of a home than where their family resided. It was not a sentiment shared by their families.

Many of the men thought that their wives didn't know about their secret trips most evenings to the shack. But they did. When pay day came and went, and their husbands still had no money, they knew. When market day came and there was no money left to buy food, they knew. When their husbands came home feeling grumpy and smelling like a beer bottle, they knew. Experience had taught them not to question their husbands about it when they came home though. So the women talked about it among themselves but not with their men. And the men didn't say anything about it because they thought it was their secret that their women didn't know about.

Each evening the shack would open its doors and men would quietly walk up the muddy path in darkness to join in the latest card game under the two bare light globes dangling from the rough cut roofing trusses and unlined corrugated iron roof. Many of the men had built up considerable *dinaus*, debts, through their losses. The generosity of the owner to continue to extend credit to them was always appreciated as each one knew that he would be able to repay the debt as soon as he made the big win. But they seemed to ignore the fact that every kina they plunged further into debt only deepened their dependence on the good will of the benefactor-owner of the establishment.

As Lupo Warina considered his options, he was well aware of the goodwill he had established with many of the men of Mambusu through their financial indebtedness to him, and the fact that he could depend on their reciprocity when the time came. He also recognised that for some of these men, public exposure of their patronage at the 'Ace Place' would place them in a serious position of shame and embarrassment, and perhaps even legal jeopardy. Certainly it would cause some grief at home for them. This would be a card he would need to play carefully though because it would also risk exposing his own interest in the illegal gambling house.

One man came to Lupo's mind. Hendros Kipa, the local businessman, a trade store owner. Hendros had managed to keep his gambling addiction hidden from the general community, and even his card playing buddies were not aware of the extent to which he had racked up debts totalling hundreds if not thousands of kina. But Lupo knew that Hendros was in serious financial difficulty following years of gambling 'misfortune', for want of a better word. He was just not a good card player, but the rush of gambling made him continue to play well beyond his own mental capacity to know when he should stop. It was exactly the weakness Lupo knew he could use to advantage - his own advantage.

The Member had his network of contacts through the community and it had been no secret that Justin Orlando had started up a trust fund or something similar and made a significant contribution to get it going. He also knew that Hendros was involved in it somehow. Hendros was his key to destroying Justin Orlando.

It was time to call in Hendros' dinau.

"Hendros, my brother, how are you today?" Lupo greeted Hendros as he called on him at his trade store, looking round quickly to make sure there were no customers there to witness the conversation.

"Member, good to see you again," replied Hendros, looking up from his counter top. He didn't mind the distraction from reading last week's Post Courier over again.

"My brother, I've come to talk to you to see if you can help me with a problem I have," said the Member.

"Member, I'm always willing to help you out, you know that," replied the businessman.

"Yes, I do know that. So what has happened is that with all this Leadership Tribunal hearing going on, I'm running out of cash for my trips to Moresby. So I need to find some additional cash."

Lupo didn't say anything more for half a minute. Hendros could see where the conversation was going, and he didn't like it.

"So, Uncle, how can I help you? You know that I don't have any cash. I have trouble giving a customer change if they have anything bigger than a 10 kina note!" said Hendros, somewhat honestly.

"Well my brother, I've been very generous in extending credit to you at our men's club, but I need you to repay the dinau now. The last time I saw, your debt was at 8,000 kina. I need to have that within the next two weeks," said Lupo, trying not to appear too demanding, yet making it very clear he was not negotiating.

Hendros looked at him, and replied, "Uncle, you know I can't repay you so quickly. Where am I going to find that sort of cash so quickly?"

"Well, I need that money and you owe it to me, so that's all there is to say," said the Member.

"What if I can't get that all to you in time then, can you give me some more time?" pleaded Hendros, knowing that the Member was also a hard businessman.

"I cannot negotiate on this, son," replied Lupo. "If you can't come up with the money within two weeks, then I may have to make news of your debt public. Your good standing in the community is at stake here, not to mention your business and marriage, so just get me the money."

Hendros stood to talk further with the Member but he was speechless, and could only watch as Lupo Warina turned around and walked towards the door. If he'd been on the street he would have seen the sly grin on Lupo's face as he walked out the door, but he didn't.

CHAPTER 11

THE FUNDS

A week had passed and it was time for the Foundation committee to meet again. I called round each of the members during the morning to arrange for us to meet in the Mambusu Guest Haus in the evening at 7pm. That would provide the most discreet venue for us to be away from unwelcome listening ears, and because Justin was already living there. Hopefully it would also be raining again and the noise of rain as well as the discomfort of standing in the rain for any eavesdroppers would mean their mission was futile.

I'd prepared some extra food in the Guest Haus kitchen. Justin and I had now been having our evening meal together at the Guest Haus so it was nice to share that with our new team.

Once everyone had arrived and we'd eaten, boiled chicken legs with rice and pumpkin and sweet potato, Justin commenced our formal Foundation committee meeting.

"Great to have everyone here and to meet together again," he welcomed. "I just want to start by reminding us of what we are here for. It's important that we continue to focus on our core purpose, our core value if you like, so we don't stray off the pathway and then not achieve our goals.

"Protecting the real gold of our community, that's what it's about. We know there's gold in the river, but we also know that there is something that is more important than that gold. It's the gold that *nenge* reminds us about, the gold of our heritage, the value of our community and the people in it. It's the value of what the Creator has given us. *Nenge* has helped us identify that this is more important than the monetary value of the river gold.

"We know that people are looking at the monetary value of the river gold and wanting to get rich from it. We also know that we will in many ways become poorer from that. Why? Because, just like what has happened in so many places around the world and in our own country, we stand to lose significant parts of our own cultural heritage in the process. For us, knowing that the *nenge* bird's primary habitat is right where the gold seam is creates an intolerable situation. If a gold mine operation starts there, it will mean the destruction of the *nenge's* habitat, and that is something which will be destructive to us as a people because we will lose that cultural foundation. *Nenge* has been the 'ridge pole' of Moiaimba cultural traditions since our first people came here. But more than that, it continues to be to this day."

I was amazed at how much of our culture Justin had discovered in even just a few months. I'd seen him out with the men earlier on as they made a new village house. He'd learnt that even though the house frame seems really shaky and wobbly while it is being constructed from its natural timber poles, there is one final element that ties it all together and creates a stable structure. When the ridge pole is tied to the top of the roof A frame with vines or 'bush rope' made from bark strips, the whole house becomes firm and solid. So we have a saying, "the strength of a community is the strength of the ridge pole". Justin had made his point well.

Justin paused and glanced to the side at me, so I continued. "That's right. Recently Uncle David told me the story of our ancestors, the first ones who came to this place. I know you are all familiar with the story but I wasn't, it was new to me." As I looked around the group I could see their gentle nods of agreement.

"All those generations ago our tribe, living on small islands somewhere in the Pacific Ocean, was nearly wiped out because of drought and famine, and because of enemy raiders who could have killed them off. They made the decision to flee from their island and find somewhere else where future generations could live in peace. That's us. We are the fruit of their decision.

"Today we are faced with a similar challenge," I continued. "We're not threatened with immediate evacuation like they were, but we are faced with changes to our *ples* and our culture which will radically change the future for our children and their children's children, the future generations that are entrusted to us. These changes will happen quickly and will be out of our control unless we can make sure that we are in control of our future. As I see it, that's what we are doing here - taking control of the future of our people."

I glanced across at Justin so he knew I'd finished saying what I wanted to say.

"Thanks Lily, you are absolutely correct. We were able to stop the Member, Honourable Lupo Warina, from his plans to bring in the South East Asian consortium to commence a mining operation under his terms, but I'm sure the glimmer of the gold will still be drawing him in, and he'll seek other ways to make it happen. So our focus is on seeking alternative ways to respect our cultural heritage, preserve the *nenge* bird's habitat, while utilising the gold to the full advantage of the community."

There was agreement between everyone in the group but David was eager to ask a question.

"Lupiano," he addressed Justin, "it seems to me that the biggest issue we need to consider today is whether you are going to stand for election in the upcoming elections or not. Can I expand a little on my thoughts here?" he asked the group, though looking at Justin. The nodding heads gave him the approval he needed.

"Well, I want to think back to the old days, at least the ones we remember, and even before that. In our tribe, the Moiaimba people, leadership has been a culturally determined appointment. What do I mean by that?" asked David. He spoke slowly, reservedly, and it was clear his wisdom was appreciated by all.

"Well, this is what I mean," he continued. "Since the first days our ancestors arrived here, *nenge* has appointed our leaders."

I couldn't contain my frustration any longer.

"Excuse me Uncle," I interrupted, "but why can't I be told about this story of the *nenge* bird? I keep on hearing about it being so important and yet no one will tell me the story. It's like you men are keeping this to yourselves and it's being kept from me. What's so important that I can't be told, or is it because I'm a woman?"

I was looking around at the rest of the committee, my eyes starting to water with the passion of my anger, but their heads were all down, eyes averted. None of them really wanted to look me in the eyes and answer my challenge. That's ok, I thought, overwhelmed by this injustice I thought I was being subjected to, I'll just wait until I get an answer.

After a few minutes of silence, when it felt like you could slice a knife through the tension between me and the men, Justin lifted his head to look me in the eyes, and spoke.

"I wish we could tell you how untrue that is Lily," Justin said softly. "There are traditions in Moi culture that form the foundation of who we are. To violate those traditions undermines the integrity of our future, of what we are to become. That is one thing we cannot afford to lose in the challenges we face at the moment."

"Lupiano is right," interjected David. "I do want to recognise the anguish you are feeling because you do not know the full story of *nenge*. But the fact of the matter is that the *nenge* bird reveals itself to those it appoints as our leaders, in a way that only those who have experienced this know. If we describe how this happens to you, then it has the opposite result and becomes like a curse - that person can never become recognised as a leader in our culture."

"Lily," added Justin, "do you remember when I told you about my grandfather's experience with Seri, your grandfather? How I read in his diary that he had shared his *nenge* experience with Seri?"

"Yes, I remember," I replied, "you said that *bubu* was cursed and could not become a leader because of this curse. But I also remember that you said that through our marriage we would break that curse by reconciling the *birua* that existed between your family and mine as a result. So the curse no longer applies, does it!"

David could see that an argument was starting between Justin and myself so he stepped into the discussion again.

"That's absolutely true Lily, that your marriage will bring reconciliation between your two lines. However, why would you want to invoke the curse on yourself by hearing the story second hand rather than have the blessing of *nenge* first hand? We want you to know the *nenge* story, but only when *nenge* reveals itself to you personally."

"That's what I keep getting told," I replied, still frustrated. "So what you are telling me is that no one is going to tell me the story, and the only way I will know it is if the *nenge* bird somehow tells me itself?"

"That's it Lily," said David.

"So tell me this, how can this bird, which for all I know may just be a figment of your imagination, a cultural hypothetical to strengthen a male dominated power base, talk to tell me?" I asked, continuing to push my point, perhaps beyond the limit.

"Lily, you will need to trust us when we tell you that however the bird reveals itself to you, you will have absolutely no doubt about its calling to you," said David graciously.

"I'm a lawyer Uncle, and I'm used to dealing in verified facts to make a judgement. You are asking me to have blind faith in what you are saying, when you can give me no proof. I'm struggling to understand this, let alone accept it."

David looked up at me again. "But as a lawyer Lily, you depend on the testimony of witnesses to determine the validity of charges. We are the witnesses who are verifying the facts to you. There are times you have to accept what others have witnessed even if you don't understand it. There will come a time when you will see for yourself, and we cannot take that initiative away from *nenge*."

In my mind I found myself thinking about another story I know, this time from the Bible, when the disciple Thomas refused to believe that the other disciples had seen Jesus alive after his death.

"Yes, like when Thomas refused to believe that Jesus was alive, despite the testimony of the other disciples, but then Jesus appeared to him as well and he believed," I said softly to myself.

My righteous anger, if I could call it that, or perhaps selfish indignation, as a better description, was dissipating.

"I'm sorry to have distracted the meeting with my unbelief, I can see how I must wait for *nenge* without doubting what you are telling me."

Justin waited for a minute and then continued with the meeting. "We accept your apology Lily, and hope that this issue resolves for you quickly. Now, David, you were saying?"

"Yes Chairman," said David, picking up the thread of his earlier thoughts. "The matter of the upcoming elections. We believe that an appointment to leadership by *nenge* is essential, and so we believe that we should support a candidate who has been appointed in this way, as you have, to represent us in parliament. Knowing as we do know that you are in fact Lupiano, following in the tradition and heritage of our people, adds strength to our desire to see you stand for the next election as our member, and with our full support. Of course the fact you have had years of experience in the public service in liaison with exploration and mining companies just adds weight to this. You are the one who knows that sector better than anyone else in the country."

I looked at Justin to see what his reaction was. We had talked very briefly about whether he should stand or not. It would not be a clean fight against Lupo Warina. He was known for his dirty tricks during campaigning. I knew that Justin felt that he hardly knew the people in his electorate as it was only a matter of months since he had come to live permanently in Mambusu. Yet he acknowledged the community support he was receiving once it was revealed that he was the rightful heir to the role of headman, Lupiano.

"Members of the committee," Justin replied, as the committee members waited in anticipation of his decision. "I have thought much about this and appreciate your support. I need another day or two to consider this before making a decision, but I'll advise you as soon as that decision is made."

The committee members breathed again, though it was clear they wanted to get on with starting their campaign for Justin.

"I have one more matter for you," said Justin. "You recall that I said I would be putting my 'going finish' pay into the Foundation account? Well, that has come through and I have a cheque here for 802,425 kina for the Treasurer to bank. We'll complete signatories on the bank account paperwork now and the Treasurer can bank the cheque immediately. Also, we'll expect monthly finance reports from the Treasurer to be presented at our meetings."

Justin held up the cheque for all to see and then stood up to present it to the Treasurer. The rest of the committee burst into applause as Justin leaned over and handed it over to Hendros Kipa.

CHAPTER 12

THE PHONE CALL

With under two months left before our wedding date, there was lots to do. Venue, food, invitations and arranging a pastor to conduct the ceremony would all take time, so I started into it by making some lists which I would talk over with Justin when we had time. It was so exciting finally seeing my dream come true - a dream I had never expected.

The biggest thing we had to plan was the arrangements for Justin's mother to come up from Sydney. So he had started the process by phoning her. Of course I was there listening in, especially when he finally got round to making the invitation to her!

"Hey Mum, I've got a surprise for you," he said, after some small talk on the phone first. "Lily and I want to invite you to a very special occasion soon."

"Don't tell me," she replied, still sharp as a tack mentally. "You're coming home! How wonderful."

"Actually, no Mum. Lily and I are getting married and we want you to come to the wedding."

"Well that's a lovely surprise, though I should have expected it, shouldn't I? Well, that is absolutely wonderful! I'm so happy for you both and can't wait to meet Lily. Will the wedding be here in Sydney then?" mother asked, sounding a little like the news was still sinking in.

"Mum, the wedding will be here in Mambusu in under two months, and we want to bring you up here for it. I'm going to come down two weeks before so I can accompany you here," said Justin in his most 'this is what's happening Mum' voice. He knew she would have her own ideas about what was best!

"Well…" she paused, "I am a bit overwhelmed to think of doing that, it's such a long way to come. But it will be wonderful to see you and meet Lily. Maybe then we can talk about you coming back to live in Sydney again," Mum said. What mother is not keen to have her children nearby?

The phone call ended after Justin said he'd call back when he had more travel details. So far so good, she hadn't declined. Justin was sure she had no idea that she was part Moiaimba and so he began to think about how he was going to break the news to her - that she would actually be the one coming home!

We laughed again about David's joke, insisting Justin spend six months in the bush to meet traditional customs before marriage. "I can't even tighten the string on a fishing line, let alone on a bow," he joked. "What hope would I have of hunting if I can't even fire an arrow!" Visions of him trying to hunt down a feral pig with only *tanket* leaves hiding his modesty made us both laugh.

One person we did need to invite, and quickly, was Kila and his family. He was Justin's former work colleague and now member of the Foundation committee. His kids called

Justin "Uncle", such was the close relationship he had with the family. It would be great to also meet Konio, Kila's wife, whom I had not met yet. I was sure the whole family would want to come up for the wedding. Justin decided to call him immediately.

"Hey brother, how are things with you?" he asked Kila. "Got the roof on your house yet?"

"Hey, my brother, good to hear from you," replied Kila. "Aw, the house is going really slowly, but we'll get there. I'm so busy at work and then weekends the boys are playing sports and just too many things to do."

"Got some good news for you. The community leaders have told us to get married in just under two months, so we want you and Konio and family to come up for a few days to join us for the wedding."

"Wow, hey, that's really cool. *Nogat tok*, we'll all be there," said Kila with real excitement in his voice. "Hey, we miss you here in Moresby, we had so much fun together, even when it was getting serious, especially with the Member." Kila knew only too well that he had stared unemployment and perhaps a prison term in the face and somehow survived when he, as Department Secretary, had double crossed the Member, Lupo Warina over the Namel Mining proposal. But now he was very firmly planted on Justin's side, and a real help in keeping his eyes and ears open to what the Member may be up to in Waigani.

"Speaking of the Member, I've got some news for you too," offered Kila. "Yeah, word is that he's still pursuing staking out a claim to gain an exploration or perhaps an alluvial licence. I don't have any details of who he is in partnership with but the boys in the office say there has been some discreet enquiries made on his behalf."

"I didn't think it would take long for him to start trying to get his hands on the gold again," replied Justin. "Let me know if you find out anything else, like what name or company he is doing this under. We need to keep one step ahead of him. What's the news on the Leadership Tribunal?" continued Justin.

"Ok, I think there is no doubt there he will be stood down for this current term. But I'm not sure if that disqualification would extend to standing for re-election. I suspect that he will be free to stand again. Have you decided if you will stand or not?" asked Kila.

"The committee is asking me the same thing. I'm still thinking it through and will make a decision soon. I want my decision to be based on what is best for the people here, not just to get the satisfaction of beating Mr Warina," explained Justin with a grin.

I was learning that he would not allow his ethical standards to drop and compromise his own morality in the process. I marvelled at these leadership qualities in him. I had to leave Justin to continue his phone call, but as I walked out the door I just managed to hear him say to Kila, "By the way, there is something I need to ask you to do."

CHAPTER 13

THE TRAP

It was time for me to catch up with some friends again. Every few weeks I'd arrange a get together with some of the other women in Mambusu. In a small community like ours, most of us had grown up together and some were relatives within our clans. Tribal relationships were forged through marriage. A person was prohibited from marrying someone from the same clan and could only marry someone from either of the other two Moiaimba clans, unless they married outside the clan altogether. In that case, the outside spouse would be adopted into a clan that was not the same as their partners. As a matrilineal society, the women retained the rights to land distribution and ownership. These rules had been set down by the very first group of survivors who reached here, though I suspect it was carried over from our earlier ancestors. Fortunately Justin and I were from different clans, something the elders would have checked first before allowing us to marry.

Our women's fellowship was structured so that we could participate in some activities together once we'd spent some time in worship and prayer. We would agree about what activity we'd do for the next meeting beforehand. There was little doubt what the women would want to do at this meeting though - wedding preparations would already have consumed their thoughts. So as the women came to the Guest Haus to meet this day, I could see they were full of ideas for food and decorations.

I think I am the last woman in the group still single, all the others are married. But sometimes that is an advantage as they feel they can trust me when they have problems in their marriage or with their children. With my legal background and understanding of law as well, it also means I can advise them legally. So I had unintentionally developed a role as a counsellor within the community, a sounding board for those who needed to talk about their family problems. I would say that I definitely knew most of the secrets of the village!

Apart from myself, the members of the Foundation committee were all men who had some standing and responsibility in the community, and I also knew their wives well. In fact the men were probably unaware of how much I knew about their personal lives, usually from times when their wives had come knocking on my door seeking advise or counsel on a problem that had come up between them and their husband.

So when Mariam entered the room with concern written all over her face, I could tell she had a problem.

"Mariam, you don't look happy today," I said as I approached her.

"Lily, I'm so worried about my husband, I can tell something is bothering him," replied Mariam.

"Have you asked him about it?" I offered.

"You know what men are like… well you will soon anyway," she said, "they keep their problems to themselves and won't say anything. He's not even talking to me about anything at the moment. It's like he's gone into a dark cave."

"Well, until he tells you what it is, why don't you put it aside in your mind and just come and enjoy our *bung*. I'm sure it will resolve itself soon."

Mariam smiled and gave a sigh. "Good idea Lily, I'm going to enjoy our time together and not let my husband's problems get in the way!" she said resolutely. "I've had some ideas about how we can decorate the Guest Haus for the wedding feast. I want this to be such a special time for all of us!"

When our devotional time was over, we started into a discussion about the wedding preparations. I could see this was going to be a huge effort by everyone. It would be the wedding of all weddings, a celebration that would go down in the history of Mambusu and the Moiaimba people. After all, it was in many ways a celebration of the return of Lupiano, the chief who had reappeared out of the *tumbuna* stories to lead his people. I was so fortunate to be chosen to be his wife.

Of course it was only natural that the discussion drifted to personal issues again and so I was not surprised when Jida started to talk with several other women about her situation.

"I wish life wasn't such a struggle," she began, "we just never have enough money to buy food and sometimes the children are hungry."

Heila butted in, "I know exactly what you mean sister, it gets so hard when we have to pay school fees and power and we don't even have enough money to be able to buy food every day. I complain to my husband about it and he just shrugs his shoulders at me."

"What I don't understand is that my husband has got a good job and yet he only gives me a couple of kina each fortnight and expects me to buy all our food with that," said Jida.

"That's happening to me as well," said Mariam as she joined the discussion.

David's wife, Joy, was in many ways a mother figure to the younger women, just as David himself was an elder for the men.

"Jida, does your husband have a regular income then?" Joy asked. "Is he getting paid each fortnight? I know he works as a government employee as the airstrip supervisor but I don't know what his wage arrangements are."

"Yes, he is paid each fortnight but I never see much of it. It seems to be nearly all gone by the time he comes home on pay day."

"Similar story for me," added Mariam. "I thought he was making a lot of money through his store, he is always bringing in new stock so must have a good turnover, but he never has enough to give me for food or school fees."

"Having no money is one thing but having a grumpy husband over fortnight weekend is another! I never look forward to pay week," added Heila.

"What do you mean Heila?" asked Joy.

"Well, he comes home late at night on pay day and is always grumpy, and usually I can smell beer on him."

I could tell by the nodding heads that there were a number of women in the group who shared this experience. I decided to find out more, to see where they felt the problem was.

"There's an issue here that we should talk about more," I suggested, and got a number of loud "yes's" from most of the women.

"Lily, many of the wives are struggling with this problem," said Heila, "and we are tired of it. We see our children suffering because they are hungry when they go to school, and sometimes our husbands even hit us when we try and talk to them about it."

"That's right, why can't they make sure we have enough money to buy food and look after all our family properly, including them?" said another woman.

"I don't know where all his money is going," said Mariam, "but I think it might have something to do with the tin shed at the top of the hill, you know, the one on the land owned by the Member's relatives. I watch him going up there often after it gets dark."

"I've seen my husband going up there as well," said Jida. Heila nodded, as did some of the other women.

"Does anyone know anything more about the tin shed?" I asked the group.

Another woman who had not spoken yet put her hand up. "I've seen that truck going there sometimes at night when it gets back from Moresby, you know, the community truck that the Member sponsored. It drives past my house to get there so I see it," she said.

"Does anyone know why the men are going there?"

Heila answered. "My husband seems to think I don't know where he goes but I do, and I think we all know that some of our husbands are going there."

"I am sorry to hear that this is such a problem for many of you," said Joy. "It's good that we talk about this and perhaps we can find a way to help each other. I'm glad that David has not got involved in it. He is always good to me and provides me enough money for our food and expenses."

"My husband doesn't smell of beer and he doesn't try to hit me, but there is something there that is taking his money away," said Mariam.

"I know what that is," said Jida with an air of certainty. "Cards. My husband always wants to gamble and he is addicted to playing cards. So I'm sure that's where his money is going."

The other woman spoke up again. "Yes, and they must be selling beer there too. If they are not gambling their money, they are wasting it on beer," she added.

I was glad the women themselves had been able to come to a conclusion about where the problem was. It was time to put on my lawyer's hat.

"So as I see it we have a problem that a number of you are facing, that is, that your husbands are spending their money on cards and beer, coming home grumpy and perhaps drunk, sometimes hitting you, and creating difficulty in your family because you don't have enough money to buy food and pay for things like school fees." I paused and looked round the group to register their agreement. Nods all round.

"So where do we go from here? What power do you women have to change this? How can we together bring about a change in our husbands?" I said, even though I didn't quite have a husband yet!

The women began to talk among themselves. Then one of them spoke.

"We need to know who is behind the tin shed, who is running this illegal business," she said.

"It looks to me like it is probably the only person who has enough money to run a shady business like this," said another. Everyone knew who she was talking about.

"Yes, and the absence of morality to do it," said another. The Member's reputation for shady deals was well known in this community!

I spoke up again. "If this person is behind the tin shed, then we can express our feelings about it at the ballot box when the time comes. But we also need a plan to drag our husbands away from it."

"I have an idea," said Mariam. "Why don't we set up a trap. You know, like when we set a trap for a bird or fish or animal. We carefully construct the trap and put it in the right place, where we know the animal will be walking, then we wait. Then…. boom…, sooner or later the animal falls into the trap!" She clapped her hands as the trap shut.

"Yeah, got him!" shouted one of the women behind me gleefully. The others laughed.

I could see the women starting to get excited about this idea, and the possibility of seeing change in their husbands.

"I'm really concerned that my husband is under some sort of pressure from the tin shed which may affect his business," said Mariam. "He is always very careful about how he runs his business, otherwise he would not be still doing it, he would have gone broke."

"I'm sure we'll get to the bottom of it, Mariam," I said. "We want to see your Hendros and all the other men becoming better husbands and fathers. We want them to fall in to our trap so they can fall out of the trap of the tin shed." There were nods of agreement all round.

"So how are we going to set this trap?" asked Jida.

CHAPTER 14

THE LOST KEY

Aihi had been driving the truck for three years now. He knew the procedure well. Arrive at Mambusu after dark, preferably after midnight when most people, hopefully no one, would see him drive into the town, and customers had gone home. Reverse up to the tin shed, remove the tarpaulin, unlock the shed door and unload the beer cartons as quickly as possible.

This night would be no different, in fact he was looking forward to finishing the job and getting home himself. Bora, his off-sider, was with him as usual, and together all went smoothly for the transfer of the refreshments into safe storage at the back of the shed. That is, until they were ready to leave. Jumping into the driver's seat, Aihi went to turn on the ignition key, but his hand reached out to nothing. The truck key was missing.

Bora was still finishing off storing cartons when Aihi called out to him.

"Hey, bush *mangi*, did you take the key?" he yelled.

Bora left what he was doing and came round to the side of the truck.

"You calling out to me?" he asked, trying to keep his voice low.

"Yeah, did you take the key out, it's not here?" yelled Aihi.

"No, why would I do that?" replied Bora. He knew Aihi always left the key in the ignition, so he must have done something with it himself.

"Well it's not here." Aihi was starting to feel annoyed. He'd never lost the key before and it was slowing things down to finish the job and get home.

"You must've taken it out, boss. Is it in your pocket?" suggested Bora respectfully.

Getting really annoyed now that his sidekick was getting mileage from his misfortune, he jumped out of the cab and stood beside Bora.

"You sure you're not playing a trick on me?" he said, pointing his finger into Bora's chest. "You are the only one who could have taken it!"

"Boss, I was in the shed so how could I have taken it? You must have taken it yourself and you can't remember!"

With his intelligence and memory now being insulted, Aihi was getting ready to thump Bora with frustration and clenched his fist. Fortunately Bora recognised his proximity to facial rearrangement, so made a practical suggestion.

"Boss, perhaps it's on the ground somewhere here. Come on, I'll help you look for it," he said.

Aihi let out a grumph, which also indicated his anger level had gone down slightly, and together they began to look round on the ground for the key. It was not so easy because they didn't want to use torches and have the light draw the attention of others who should not know they were there.

It took a few minutes but near the back of the truck they finally found the key, just lying on the ground, as Bora had suggested.

"Ok, let's just get out of here," instructed Aihi.

"But I didn't finish stacking the boxes, boss," replied Bora.

"Leave them, they're in the shed, that's all we need to do. Shut the shed door and let's get out of here."

Bora quickly raced back to shut the shed door, and the two of them jumped into the cab and drove off without looking back. If they had, they may just have seen the side of a woman's face peering through the door, now very slightly open. What they would not have seen is the smile on her face, from ear to ear!

Jida waited until the truck was well out of sight, and then waited a few more minutes before opening the door fully. Three other women appeared out of the darkness, carrying plastic buckets. Once inside the shed, they shut and locked the door.

"Who has the bottle opener?" she asked quietly as another woman lit two candles.

Mariam was giggling to herself and could hardly contain herself. "I put a whole packet of salt into each bucket of water," she giggled proudly. The others all started to laugh with her. For just a brief moment they enjoyed the hilarity before the first bottle top flipped off with a 'pop'.

"I'll check the playing cards," said Heila. Again restrained laughter.

Next day there was an unusual smell coming from Heila's *haus kuk* fire. The smell of burning playing cards. Ace's, to be exact.

CHAPTER 15

THE RESCHEDULE

I'd continued my work as Receptionist at the Mambusu Guest Haus, which was great because Justin was living there and so we got to see each other often during the day. I enjoyed coming to work each morning and to be greeted by him.

"Hi beautiful," he greeted me with today.

"You're such a teaser - you know that I'm working and can't flirt with the clients!" I said with a fake straight face. I walked purposely over to the reception desk and started to prepare the paperwork for the day.

"Oh, so I'm a client now?" teased Justin. "What happened to the fiancé?"

"Oh, him… I decided I could live without him for a day," I teased back, pretending to ignore him.

It didn't work and I couldn't stop smiling as he started to walk over to me, looking very serious.

"Excuse me, Miss Receptionist," he said when he got to the counter. I paused for a second while I got rid of my smile and looked up at him again.

"Yes Sir, is there something I can help you with today?" I asked in my best receptionist voice.

"I want to make a complaint to the manager," he said, also trying to be official.

"Certainly Sir," I replied, "and what might the complaint be?"

"Well, up until today the receptionist has continually flirted with me. In fact, whenever she comes in she usually greets me with a hug. She is always so happy and chatty to see me."

"Well Sir, I can see that *that* behaviour is totally inappropriate and I will make sure the Manager is aware of it," I said, being serious.

"Thank you Miss," continued Justin. "My complaint is a very serious one and it is this. She didn't do this when she came in today and just treated me like a normal client!"

I started to grin, trying to hide it, but couldn't. "Well Sir, I'll make sure the Receptionist rectifies that situation immediately."

We both burst into laughter as I came out from behind the counter and into his arms. How I loved this man!

"Actually I do have something serious to talk with you about," said Justin.

I took a step back to listen.

"We need to discuss it more with the Foundation committee but I think the idea about applying for an alluvial licence is a good one, and something we should start doing quickly. What I'm thinking is that we should plan to get back up to the gold vein area soon and survey it in preparation for the application."

This was one of the options we'd discussed earlier, that the community hold an alluvial licence for the area around the gold vein and the river. This would allow locals and perhaps tourists the opportunity to pan for gold, thus contributing back directly into the economy of the community, while blocking attempts by others to apply for a full scale mining licence.

"I agree with you," I replied, "I think the way things have been moving so fast, and the way Mr Warina keeps pushing with his agenda for a mine, we do need to keep moving to give some sort of security to the areas where the gold is found."

"Yes, and that also gives some security for the *nenge* bird's habitat," said Justin. "Well, let's plan to go up to the site the week after next. We may need to camp up there for one or two nights. I think my leg and foot will be strong enough to handle the walk there again".

"I'll get together what we need for the trip then," I said. "I can't wait to get back there again under happier circumstances. You know I haven't been back since we found you there after the airplane accident."

My mind raced back to the scene, still etched indelibly on my mind. Justin, lying on the stones beside the river with his ankle smashed, in agony and exhausted. He'd extricated himself from the aircraft after the crash the previous day and dragged himself down to the river. Another memory came, the fact that he was still in such good spirits. Something had happened that had profoundly affected him and it seemed to be something to do with the *nenge* bird which lives in the same area. It only increased my desire to discover the mystery of this bird for myself. But how could I make that happen? Perhaps visiting the area again for the survey will give me some answers?

With our wedding now only weeks away, Justin had decided that he should go to Sydney a few days earlier than planned to give himself time to debrief his mother and convince her to come back with him. He was pretty unsure if she would really decide to come. She'd never mentioned her PNG past and Justin was sure that she was not aware of the fact that she was part Moiaimba. In fact he reckoned that she had not been told anything about her history, coming out from PNG in the first year or two of her life with his grandfather.

I have to say, I wasn't very happy with Justin about this decision of his to go earlier. I'd been planning to conduct the survey of the river and gold vein area and now had surveyors booked to join us to do it. We'd agreed that getting this survey done soon was essential so we could submit our application for an alluvial licence. But if Justin was going to hike off to Australia then it left me to do the survey by myself. Besides, I was going to miss him even though it would only be for about two weeks. I was starting to feel overwhelmed, so I cornered Justin at the Guest Haus when he came in next.

He could see there was something bothering me the moment he walked in.

"Hey, what's up? You look a bit stressed," he said.

"Well actually, I'm more than a bit stressed," I replied, "I'm starting to feel a bit overwhelmed by everything that's going on. You know, we have a wedding in a couple of weeks, you want the survey done, and the alluvial application in as soon as possible, and now you are going away in the middle of it…"

"Whoa… ," said Justin as he took a deep breath. "I thought you would love being fully involved in doing these things."

"There's just too much happening at once and I can't do it alone, especially when you're not here," I countered. "Can't you do something?"

We talked a bit more until we finally decided to see what changes to our schedule we could make. The final result looked like this: Justin would go down to Sydney for a week and bring his mother back and she could have 2 weeks with us before the wedding. We would schedule the survey for immediately after he got back and I would be able to spend the week he was away doing wedding preparations. I was happy with this.

Justin changed his flights out of Port Moresby for Sydney to suit the new plan, and a few days later he called me from Sydney.

"Hey, I have to tell you the most amazing thing happened here," his excitement electrifying.

"Go on, tell me."

"Well, I spent the evening with Mum after I got here yesterday. You know I've been wondering how I might introduce this whole topic of her PNG heritage."

"So did you tell her?" I interjected.

"We had the most amazing conversation I've ever had with her. It was unbelievable," said Justin.

"Well… go on, tell me what happened," I said, a little agitated.

"Well, she knew," he said.

"What, she knew?"

"Yes, she knew. She let me tell her about her having a PNG mother, me thinking I was telling her some new mystery about her life, and she just sat there calmly listening. Then when I had finished I looked up at her and there were tears in her eyes. She already knew, but I don't think she knows the full story," said Justin.

"Wow," I said quietly, "that's amazing." I could feel the tears welling up in my own eyes now. I needed to know more, but for the moment we were both silent, unable to speak.

Justin's voice was wavering when he finally spoke again.

"She just looked me in the eye through her tears and said she'd been waiting for this moment all her life. I can't wait to tell her the full story when we get back and she can hear the story from your side too."

CHAPTER 16

THE DINAU

It came as a surprise next day when the word got out that the Member, Honourable Lupo Warina, had arrived in Mambusu. Accompanied by a small group of men and surveying equipment, it was obvious he meant business. A number of townsfolk still gathered at the Guest Haus carpark to welcome him, not concerned that he was suspended and under investigation by the Leadership Tribunal.

Warina knew that there would be spies among those who had gathered so he was deliberately vague about his intentions. Of course he was right. David Umbare happened to be nearby and heard the crowd gathering so he joined them. Nudging his way through the group, he made sure he was in earshot of the Member. It wasn't long before someone posed the inevitable question.

"What are you going to do here, Member?"

"Well as you all know, I am fully committed to the welfare of our community and so I've arranged for some survey work to be done in the community. This will enable us to move forward with infrastructure development that is well overdue," replied the Member.

"Where will you be surveying?" asked another onlooker.

"There's a number of locations we'll be considering," said the Member, deliberately keeping his hearers in ignorance.

For David Umbare, who knew more than anyone else what was going on in his community, the warning bells started to ring. He knew there was no plan for any surveying on the books for Mambusu town. So there was only one place the Member would be going to - the gold vein.

Within a few minutes Umbare had left the group and come into the Guest Haus. He looked worried.

"What's the matter Uncle?" I asked. He was looking at the floor and shaking his head. I knew it must be serious because of all the people I knew, he was the most unflappable. Nothing seemed to bother him, but now was different.

"I think we are in trouble Lily." He paused for a second before continuing. "The Member is here, with a survey team."

My heart skipped a beat as I started to take in what he had said. Our plans to survey the area next week when Justin returned, in preparation to apply for an alluvial licence, may suddenly be in jeopardy if the Member has the same intention. Suddenly the world had changed - the race to get an alluvial licence was now on.

We stood together in silence for some time, both of our minds racing to keep up with this latest development.

I was the first to speak. "What are we going to do, Uncle?"

"I really don't know, we should talk to Justin. But it seems that the Member is a week ahead of us and so if we can't do something to get ahead of him, he'll be the one with the alluvial licence, not us."

"I'll ring Justin now," I said, and went to get my mobile phone from the Guest Haus office.

"Hi beautiful," said Justin as he answered my phone call. "I wasn't expecting you to call so soon. What's happening?"

"I've got some bad news. The Member is here with a survey team, though he's not saying what they are here to do. But Uncle David and I think he must be preparing to also apply for an alluvial licence. How did he know we would be doing a survey next week?"

"Wow," was all Justin could say at first. "It does look like that's what the Member is up to. What are your thoughts about what we should do?" he asked.

"Lupiano, what choice do we have but to get our survey done this week and get our application in to Moresby hopefully before the Member does. But the Member has a big start ahead of us, we'll have to pull out all stops to get down to the site before him," offered Umbare.

"I think you are right Uncle, if we can't beat the Member with our application then all our hopes are nothing. He will use an alluvial licence to his own benefit while he gets together another mining consortium to expand to a full mine," said Justin.

I knew in my heart what this meant - we would have to do the survey before Justin came back to Mambusu from Sydney. My worst nightmare was unfolding and I felt overwhelmed.

"Lily, do you think you can get our surveyors out tomorrow and get down to the gold site as soon as possible?"

"But I thought we agreed that we'd do the survey when you got back," I blurted back.

"Well we did, but things have changed. We have to respond to this or we lose everything we have been working towards. Not just us but the whole community."

I could see there was no point arguing now, I needed to step up and do what was needed - by myself.

"I know you can do this," added Justin.

"Ok," I replied, "I'll call them now to come out from Moresby tonight so we can get down to the site first thing in the morning."

After I'd hung up the phone, I sat down to start planning what I needed to do tonight in preparation for the trek to the gold site. One of the uncertainties on my mind was the weather. While the wet season was on the way out, there were still heavy rain storms some days and nights. That made the river treacherous to cross. So I would need to plan carefully to be able to safely cross the river at the right time and in the best place.

I called Kila to let him know what was happening and then arranged with the surveyors to drive out this afternoon or evening to be ready to go down to the gold site first thing in the morning.

"Daughter," said Umbare David, "I'll arrange a couple of the young men to accompany you tomorrow and they can also assist the surveyors. We may need to be ready to clear some patches of bush away for them to be able to use their survey equipment and get the sightings they need. Take enough food for a couple of days too because you know the river can easily be flooded when it rains, cutting you off from getting home."

"Thanks Uncle, that will be a great help," I replied, though my thoughts were now on other preparations. "Oh, by the way, did you happen to hear anything about the Member's schedule, like when he is planning to go down to the river?"

"No, unfortunately he wasn't giving away any information when he spoke to people, so we just have to move as fast as we can and expect he will be close, hopefully behind us and not in front of us!"

"I think we'll leave before dawn then and try and get the advantage," I said. "Can you tell the others to be ready for 5 am?"

That afternoon, the Member took the opportunity to pay a visit to some of his friends in the community. It was important not only that he was seen to be active in the community, but that he was able to maintain his interests responsibly. That usually meant calling on those people who owed him something, or had done something to upset him.

First port of call was his shopkeeper friend, Hendros Kipa. He knew Hendros would not be expecting to see him in person.

"Hey, my brother, how is business going today," he said as he marched into Hendros' tradestore. "Was just in town for some other business and thought I'd drop by."

Hendros was reading yesterday's National newspaper on his front counter when he heard the MP's voice and looked up to see him confidently entering the store. It crossed Hendros' mind that the MP always seemed to visit when he had no other customers in the store.

"Uncle, good to see you again," responded Hendros, trying hard to maintain an upbeat voice but knowing he may have failed. After his last encounter with the Member, and the financial pressure he was now under, he had wished to never see the MP again!

"Yes, indeed, my brother. So how is business in the store going? I was hoping it might pick up a lot so that you can meet your obligations to me."

Hendros could feel the knife edge of blackmail digging deeper into his heart.

"Not really, Uncle, you know, nothing much changes in Mambusu."

"So do I take it that you are no better off now than you were last time we talked?" suggested the Member.

"I'm afraid so," said Hendros, "as I said before, I just don't have that sort of money. You have put me in an impossible situation." Hendros' thoughts began to go back into the nightmare situation he was now in - if he couldn't pay the debt, Warina was going to expose his gambling problem. The shame with his family and community would destroy him and his business.

"We'll, I'm going to give you another two days. I'm going down to the gold vein tomorrow to do some survey work and when I get back I want to see cold hard cash. You know that as a politician I always keep my promises, and I will keep this one."

The Member stood looking at Hendros, who had nothing but a deep frown on his face. Hendros was expecting him to leave but then he wanted to talk about something else.

"By the way, what happened at the Ace Place the other night?" he asked. "I heard there was a little bit of trouble but I'm not clear about what happened. Do you know anything about it?"

Happy to get off the topic of his *dinau*, Hendros wondered how much he should disclose. He didn't want to be implicated on another matter which had upset the Member.

"I'm really not sure, Uncle. There was something funny about the cards and we were all having a terrible game. We eventually worked out that there were no Ace's in the packs.

I don't know how that happened. Then some of the boys, a bit later in the night, started to throw up after swallowing a mouthful of salty water."

"Why were they drinking salty water, that's a bit strange, there was plenty of beer."

"No Uncle, you see some of the beer bottles only had salt water in them, not beer," advised Hendros.

"Salt water instead of beer? That's really strange don't you think? So what do you think happened? How did the cards and beer bottles get changed?" The Member was using very direct questioning which agitated Hendros, like the Member was accusing him.

"I don't know, Uncle, but it certainly looks like someone was sabotaging the shed," suggested Hendros.

The Member thought for a minute and then said, "Who would do that? It must be someone who is unhappy with the shed, or unhappy with the owner, which is me. Do you know anyone who would want to pay me back for something?"

Hendros could feel the heat of accusation now - did the Member suspect that he, Hendros, may have had a part to play in the sabotage?

"I'll be doing a full investigation when I return and whoever did this will pay for it, I can assure you of that." With that, the Member turned round and walked back out of the trade store.

A bewildered Hendros began to weigh up his options once more, but, once again, found he had none. In a few days his life would be destroyed when the Member fulfilled his promise to expose him in the community. It was a sad predicament, as it always is when you know you've done wrong and have to face the punishment of your wrongdoing.

His eyes now glanced over to the book lying on his desk, the Foundation's bank deposit book.

The Member's next visit was to his old friend and truck driver, Aihi. He hadn't contacted his old friend to tell him he was visiting Mambusu, so Aihi would be surprised to see him. But better to catch him off guard than have him try to prepare an alibi. In the Member's mind, Aihi must have been in on the sabotage - but pity anyone who tries to double cross Lupo Warina!

Aihi was outside his house on the edge of Mambusu, working on his truck brakes. One front wheel was lying on the ground and brake pads and other parts were scattered around on the ground near the wheel. An old hydraulic jack was supporting the front axle while Aihi wrestled with a spanner, hands covered in dirt and brake fluid. He looked up as he saw the Member approaching.

"Ah Member, this is a surprise, I wasn't expecting to see you for another few weeks, but welcome back to Mambusu," said Aihi enthusiastically, not anticipating the fire of anger that might burn him shortly. One look at the Member's face though changed that.

"My brother, I need to talk with you," greeted the Member, "NOW!"

Aihi felt the overbearing presence of the Member towering over him as he lay sprawled on the ground. He recognised the need to act calmly - the Member's reputation was well known. Carefully putting his spanner down, Aihi rose to his feet to at least be at eye level with the Member.

"Member, what would you like to talk to me about?" said Aihi. He'd heard about the problems at the shed the other night but it had nothing to do with him.

The Member got straight to the point. "Did you sabotage my operation? I've received reports of salt water in beer bottles, and card packs with no Ace card. You are the one delivering the beer, and you are the only one who has access to the shed apart from my duty manager, who says he knows nothing about it. So what's the story?"

"I know nothing about it, Member. I just deliver the goods after everyone has gone to bed, and get out of there, just as you are paying me to do," replied Aihi, feeling the indignation of this false accusation against him.

"You are lying to me. You are the only one who can unlock the door, so give it to me straight. What happened?" replied the Member, pointing his finger at Aihi.

"No, no, no Member, you are not going to pull that stunt on me. I am not lying. I know nothing about it. We delivered the goods as arranged and left."

The events of recent evenings were going through his mind when suddenly he remembered the key. There was something unusual one night, the truck key was missing, and they found it on the ground. He was just about to open his mouth and tell the Member about it, but reconsidered. If he told the Member, it would create a situation of uncertainty in his mind which would only create more suspicion - and that suspicion would not help Aihi's cause. So he said nothing.

"You see, brother, since that night, business has plummeted," lamented the Member. "The boys are not coming anymore. I can't be providing a service to the men in the community when people are sabotaging me. I can't afford to buy any more beer stocks now, my business is ruined. That means your job is on the line too. I need to know answers, and mark my word, I will punish those responsible!"

"Like I said, Member, I know nothing about it," replied Aihi, determined not to get dragged into the blame, "I've just been doing my job. Besides, I don't have any reason to want to sabotage you, do I? You've always looked after me well so I have no complaints."

The Member looked at Aihi for a minute in silence, then turned his back and left.

CHAPTER 17

THE CONFESSION

Sometimes people knocked on the door of the Mambusu Guest Haus before entering, sometimes not. But if they wished to be a little more secretive when visiting me, as some of the women were when they came to talk about their personal lives - and husbands - they would give a short cough outside the window. I could then signal to them to know if I already had visitors in the Guest Haus, or if it was clear for them to come in so we could talk privately.

So it was that a worried Hendros Kipa, Treasurer of the Foundation committee, found himself outside my window coughing. I waved through the window for him to come in. He looked so worried, his face tormented. I guessed that he had not been home for some time as he wouldn't want his wife to see how he was feeling.

"Hendros," I greeted him at the Guest Haus door, "Come in. You look so worried, what's the matter?"

"I need to let you know something. The Member just visited me and told me that he was going down to the gold place to do surveying. I thought I should come and tell you. I think he's up to no good again."

"Yeah, that's what we are all thinking. We suspected that he's going to do a survey to submit for an alluvial gold licence. I'm surprised he told you as he must know you are on the Committee. It does confirm what we suspected."

"Does Lupiano know? What can we do about it?" asked Hendros.

"Yes, I phoned Justin a little while ago. We have no choice but to try and get down there before the Member does and get our application in first."

Hendros noticed the apprehension in my voice. "I thought you didn't want to go on your own?"

"I didn't, but it looks like I have no choice with Justin still in Australia."

"If you ask me then," said Hendros, "I think you will be ok. Have you got some others going with you?"

"Yes," I replied, "Uncle David has arranged for some of the boys to come and they can help clear the bush for the surveyors. I called them too and they'll be arriving late this afternoon ready to leave at 5 am. I know that it will be ok but I'm still nervous about it," I confided.

I noticed Hendros was carrying something, then saw that it was the Foundation's bank record book.

"How did you go banking that huge cheque?" I asked, looking at the bank book in his hand.

"Yeah, ok, the funds cleared today." He seemed to be very unexcited about it, like it actually wasn't ok. My years of dealing with people had given me the ability to perceive when people were being bothered by something. Perhaps that's why

I had a steady stream of people from the community coming to me for counsel?

I put my hand on Hendros' shoulder. "Something else seems to be bothering you. Do you want to talk about it?" I gently asked him.

At first he shook his head, but I could see the tears starting to well up in his eyes. He was in serious trouble, I could tell. I stayed there with him, just giving him time to open up.

After a little while he started to get his thoughts in order, enough to tell me about it. "I don't know what to do. I'm in a situation that I can't get out of. My wife won't like it, and my reputation in the community and my business are all about to be ruined. It could ruin the Foundation too. My life is in a mess. I don't know what to do." The man was broken.

"You can tell me about it if you want to."

"I… I….I've been playing cards in the evenings at the shed. My wife doesn't know about it." He paused. I just nodded to let him know that I was listening.

"It's worse than that. I've had a lot of losses and have a big *dinau* to the shed boss. Now he wants his money back and is threatening to expose me if I don't pay, by tomorrow." The look of desperation on his face increased. "I'm going to lose everything."

He'd said all he wanted to for the moment. We sat together in the guest in silence before I asked him, "Do you have any options?"

"The only option I have is to use Foundation fund money to pay the *dinau*," he confessed. Is that why he was carrying the bank book I wondered?

"Have you taken that money then," I asked.

"It has been the most difficult experience of my life, Lily. Here in my hands I have the solution to my problems. K8,000 is such a small amount out of this money, I'm sure it would not be noticed."

The temptation to steal from the Foundation fund was huge, but I wanted him to tell me what he did, so I waited silently for him to finish his story.

"I went to the bank agency on the way here. The cheque funds have been cleared. I walked in the door but then realised that I could not let the Committee down. For all the bad things I have done to land me in this situation, I could not let you all down by stealing from the fund. That would only make things worse. So I decided I must face up to my gambling problem and deal with it, and not add stealing to my collection of wrongdoings. So here I am now. Take the bank book from me because tomorrow my name and reputation will be mud."

I looked into his eyes. There was relief mixed with desperation. But there is always relief when we own up to our failures and tell someone else we can trust.

"Uncle, I want to tell you several things. First of all, your good wife does know about the shed. All the wives do. She has longed for you to give it up but has waited patiently for that to happen. Today will be the happiest day of her life."

Hendros looked up at me with surprise. "You mean, she knows?"

"Yes, she knows where you go. She knows about the cards and the money she never gets to buy food and clothes for the children. She'll forgive you when you confess it to her, and she won't judge you when you are honest with her. She just wants you back again, without the gambling."

Hendros began to weep as this revelation became clear.

"What a fool I've been," he mumbled, "I'm so sorry."

"You need to say that to your wife," I said.

"I'm still ruined by this *dinau* to the Member. He is going to destroy me if I can't pay it."

We sat together in silence for a few minutes once again. The Member knew that this experience for Hendros would be so destructive to all that they were seeking to do in the community. They must find a way to avert it.

"Uncle, I have an idea. Let me ring Justin first and talk with him. Can you give me a few minutes? Would you like a coffee while you wait, I'll get you one first?"

Hendros nodded and slumped into one of the Guest Haus lounge chairs. I fetched a fresh cup of coffee for him from the kitchen before phoning Justin.

"Hey Lily, this is a surprise, two calls in two hours!" said Justin.

"Wish you were back here, there is too much happening and I'm feeling like its getting out of control," I replied.

"Oh, what's happening now?"

"Well Uncle Hendros has been told by the Member that he wants his *dinau* of K8,000 back from Hendros tomorrow. Hendros has just told me that he's had a gambling problem playing cards at the shed and the Member will expose him to the community if he doesn't pay up…"

"Hang on, let's slow down and back up a little," interrupted Justin. "What's the shed and why is the Member chasing a gambling *dinau* from Hendros?"

"Well," I continued, "the Member runs an illegal gambling and drinking operation for the local men in the shed on the edge of town, you know, the tin shed at the top of the hill. The Member must be running out of money because he's wanting Hendros to pay back his gambling debt and threatening exposure if he doesn't. Hendros is fearful it will ruin him. He thought his wife didn't know but she does."

Justin was thinking through the scenario that was emerging. "I wonder if the Member thought he could use this situation to disrupt the Foundation? Hendros may be tempted to use Foundation fund money to pay the *dinau*."

"Yes, exactly. Hendros just confessed to me that he nearly did do that. The man is broken, Justin, he's in a real mess about this and doesn't know what to do. But he didn't use the money and has just given the bank book back to me. He's ready to accept the consequences of the Member exposing his gambling problem."

"Oh I'm so glad to hear that he didn't steal the money. That is the mark of a good man who knows, despite the temptation, what the right thing to do is. Let me think about this for a minute."

"Yes. I wondered if we could actually use Foundation money to help him through this?" I suggested.

A few moments later Justin was back on the phone. "First of all, can you affirm Hendros and pat him on the back for his integrity in not taking Foundation money to pay his *dinau*. Tell him that we trust him and want him to continue as Treasurer, and give him back the bank book. He needs to know that this experience has only confirmed our trust in him. We know he is trustworthy."

"Ok, I'll tell him that straight away," I replied. "I think it will blow him away, that we are actually prepared to trust him more after this!"

"That's great. I've got another idea, but I think you thought of it first. See what you think about this," said Justin. "It will need approval of all the committee but we can arrange for that easily."

"Ok, I'm open for anything because we are out of ideas at this end," I replied.

"What if we arrange a loan of the funds Hendros needs from the Foundation, all legally written up, and a repayment schedule for Hendros to pay back to the Foundation? He does have a debt which he has to pay, but if we can help him, that way the Member no longer has power over him, and any attempt to undermine the Foundation has been negated."

"Wow, that would be an amazing way to resolve it," I said. "I'll get round the rest of the committee and see if we can make that happen. Hendros will be beside himself to be free from the Member's blackmail."

Once again I recognised the wisdom that Justin had in thinking through solutions which could turn a negative into a positive. I guess that's why the *nenge* bird recognised him as Lupiano.

I left Hendros at the Guest Haus, without telling him about the call with Justin yet, or giving him back the bank book, while I visited the other committee members at their homes or work place. All were in agreement with Justin's suggestion as the best way forward, and in positively encouraging brother Hendros as he now dealt with his gambling problem. As I still had the bank book in my hand, I called into the bank agency and withdrew the money ready to hand to Hendros.

When I got back to the Guest Haus, Hendros had got himself a second cup of coffee and was looking a little more relaxed, though still worried about the *dinau*.

"I've got some good news for you," I announced, handing

the bank book back to him. He was reluctant to take it but I insisted.

"The committee members all want to thank you for not touching the Foundation's funds. We are all united in wanting to support you to deal with your gambling problem. We are all on your side, so we want you to know that we trust you as Treasurer."

A look of relief and confusion spread across his face. He was accepted by the group even though they knew about his problem.

"Secondly, we want to help you with a solution to your debt with the Member. Therefore we are unanimous in offering you a loan of the amount needed so you can pay the Member and get him off your back. We believe he may be trying to use your *dinau* to disrupt us. You have stopped that happening by not stealing any of our funds. So we will use those funds with a legal loan to you."

I held out an envelope with the money in it and invited him to take it. Slowly, as he realised what he was being offered, he reached out and accepted the envelope.

"I can't believe this is happening." This time the tears were of joy and release. "I came here broken and in despair and you have offered me not only encouragement and hope, but the very means by which I can solve this. I can't believe it is happening. I am so grateful. Thank you."

"I'll write up a formal loan agreement with you now and then I need to get back to preparing for tomorrow. But you need to get back to your wife now and talk with her."

Hendros looked at me, the relief and joy so evident now. He had received grace instead of judgement and all he had was thankfulness. He grabbed my hand to shake and then left to talk to his wife.

CHAPTER 18

THE RACE

I was glad that it wasn't raining when I woke at 4 am. The survey crew and the boys coming with me started turning up at the Guest Haus soon after 4.30 am ready for the hearty breakfast of taro and sweet potato and cup of hot tea I'd promised them, before heading off to the river.

Many of the team were very familiar with the landscape down to the river and up to the gold site. Years of hunting in the area had proven the best tracks through the bush and across the Bright River, which had no bridge, unlike the first river. I remembered so vividly the last time I crossed that single file wire bridge with timber slats a few months ago. The boys were struggling to carry Justin across on a bush stretcher after we rescued him from his airplane accident with a broken ankle. Why am I thinking of him already?

Down the mountain side from Mambusu we trekked in the dark, making as little noise as we could to avoid being heard by our enemies. We used the torches sparingly and only pointing downwards, again to avoid being seen. In single file we marched down the track until we reached the wire bridge, then across it to the land inside the fork of the rivers, where the two joined to one to flow to the ocean.

Over breakfast we'd planned our route well. Speed was of the essence and the sooner we could get there, conduct the survey needed, and return, the better. A sense of urgency permeated the group now and no one wasted any time or energy that would otherwise help our trek. We all knew that we had a good six or seven hours of walking ahead of us and we wanted to make good progress while we were fresh. I'd packed a few things into my backpack, making sure it wasn't heavy enough to weigh me down and slow us up - a change of clothes, a small waterproof sheet which could provide shelter from the rain and some food items, including a couple of packets of Chicken flavoured noodles and two tins of tuna, as well as water and a sharp knife and other eating utensils. I figured we would be able to find some fresh vegetables along our way as well. There were a couple of places where sweet potato had been grown earlier on and some of the boys knew where they were. Machetes and axes and matches were standard hiking kit for the boys, so we'd easily be able to make a fire to cook and keep warm by.

By 7 am the sun was well and truly up and we stopped for a short rest. Looking through the jungle canopy though, we could see that it was actually a cloudy day. We all recognised what that meant - the high probability of rain. We must keep moving then.

As we were shouldering our back packs again, one of the village men called out.

"Hey, come and look at this!"

Walking over to him, we saw a worried look on his face. While these bush tracks were regularly well used by people hunting or going to food gardens, and so we had not taken much notice of other footprints, our colleague had seen something.

"Look at these foot prints," he said. "I think they are fresh, like in the last 2 hours. If you look carefully you'll see a set of boot prints that are new. I don't know anyone in Mambusu who has that kind of boot."

"That's right, they don't sell that shoe in Mambusu so it must be someone who has just come in from outside," said another.

"Who do you think it could be?" another asked me.

"I don't think there is any doubt about who it might be," I answered. "He must have got started before we did and is now well ahead of us."

The sense of urgency now tripled! We had to try and catch up with them and overtake them - without them knowing! Now that the boys had their scent, we would follow their trail until we knew we could take a shorter route - or risk running into them!

We quickened our pace as we set off again. The now narrow track was muddy from lots of recent travellers and the undergrowth scratched past us at every step. By 10 am we were exhausted and agreed to stop again for a short break. Backpacks were quickly thrown to the ground, followed immediately by their owners, glad to get off their feet for a few minutes. Someone had gathered some *laulau* fruit from a tree on the way and that was shared round.

The boys who had first seen the boot prints did another scan around. "We think they are not far away now," they said. "Their tracks are very fresh, perhaps only 15 or 30 minutes ago."

I knew we were approaching the river and so we'd need to find the best place to cross it. There were a number of crossing places. Some had logs across more narrow sections, others were shallow and wide and could be waded across at knee height. The next hour could prove to be the difference between overtaking our enemies or not, depending on which river crossing we decided on.

Knowing they were not too far in front of us now, we decided to take a more dangerous but potentially quicker route which crossed the river over several fallen trees.

"I suspect that the Member will not be travelling as fast and his boots are probably full of water and leeches by now anyway," I said. There were grins and laughs all round. He was probably not as prepared as they were for a long jungle walk - pacing the offices of Parliament House in Waigani in dress shoes was not quite the same!

"What crossing do you think he will take?" I asked the group. After a few minutes discussion one of them volunteered their wisdom.

"We reckon he'll travel further up on this side and then take the shallow crossing so he can just wade across." I remembered this crossing as the one we took when bringing Justin back from the crash site. There I go, thinking of Justin again!

"Ok, let's expect that then, and make our plans based on that. We'll take the 'three logs crossing' just up ahead here, and continue on the other side of the river. Hopefully we can get there before they do and surprise them," I said. No one seemed to have any problem about me calling the shots - I was definitely the boss!

The 'three logs crossing' had barely changed for many years and our party quickly scrambled across the logs, now well worn from travellers. Into the bush on the other side we disappeared and were once again established on a narrow track paralleling the river, taking us to the gold site. We reckoned we needed another two hours of walking to reach it. That is, if the rain didn't slow us down.

We'd noticed a light drizzle starting as we neared the 'three logs crossing' and it was not long before it had developed into a gentle but steady downpour. It made for a muddy walk as the depressions in the pathway caused by walkers now filled with water. We didn't mind walking in the rain. In the middle of the day it wasn't so cold. But we all realised that we didn't have a warm house to return to tonight, just whatever shelter we could manage to make from bush materials and our waterproof sheets.

Another hour and we knew we were approaching the place where the shallow river crossing led into the jungle. The rain had intensified and I knew we were in for a wet night.

"I can hear voices," whispered the lead walker of the group. We crawled through the bush for about twenty metres so that we were perched on the river bank and could see across the river. There were voices all right, and one we immediately recognised. Soon the Member and his party emerged onto the stoney bank on the other side of the river. There was some discussion going on but we couldn't make out the words. It probably related to the fact that the river had risen slightly with the rain, and the member was going to get more than his knees wet. No one was volunteering to carry him though!

As we secretly watched from the other side, hidden in the jungle, the Member's three surveyors stepped into the water and started to cross over. The river was about 50 metres wide at this point, mainly small rocks with a few larger ones scattered here and there. The constantly moving rocks underfoot meant that you could not hurry across but needed to carefully secure each foothold as you went. It took time.

Once the three surveyors were on their way across the river, the Member and a couple of his helpers entered the water, carefully picking their way across step by step. The last thing the Member wanted was to loose his foothold and find himself upended but completely soaked in less than a metre of water!

We'd decided to move upstream of the crossing so that we were in front of the Member's party. Knowing that it would take them a little while to gather together once they crossed, and that they would not be aware that we were now ahead of them, we could continue the last section well in front of them.

As we peered through the bush at them, fern leaves stuck in our hair as camouflage, I heard a sound. At first it was barely distinguishable from the rain, which had continued to increase in intensity. But gradually it became louder through the rain. And I knew exactly what it was.

The Member and his team had heard the sound too. At first confused by it, they were now in no suspicion about what it was. A flash flood. The roar increased as the torrent of water rushed down the river towards them.

I knew that we were not safe either as we were too close to the river bank. We needed to get out of harm's way - but needed to see what would happen to the Member and his team. We yelled out to them, revealing ourselves. Their lives were now more important than our mission.

"Get out of the water quickly, the flood is coming!" we yelled at the top of our voices. I don't think they heard us over the noise of the rain and water but I needed to watch them for as long as I could before running away from the river and up to higher ground.

The surveyors, now in the middle of the river, had swung around and were trying desperately to run across the stoney under-surface, tripping and stumbling often. They dumped their equipment into the river to lighten their load. The Member was also trying to get back to the river bank but his heavy boots, full of water, were no help to him. Just as he reached the bank, the flood came round the corner, a foaming mass of water and foliage about three metres high.

We watched as the three surveyors were swept away, disappearing into the foamy mass in an instant. The last we saw of the Member was his desperate attempt to run up the river bank to higher ground. The water enveloped him and I saw him struggling to keep his head out of it as the water swirled him round. At least he was on the river's edge and had a chance to survive if he could struggle to the shore. The surveyors had no chance at all. Until we could cross the river again, there was nothing we could do to help him.

The rest of my team had already run off to get to higher ground. I knew I could stay no longer or I would risk being caught up in the water as it rose. I took off, away from the river, punching through the soaked jungle as best I could to desperately reach higher ground. Leaves and vines slashed across my face and arms and legs, stinging me, but I didn't care. I was in a race for life.

Once I knew I was a safe distance from the river, I turned to follow the river up towards the gold site again. I'd lost the path though, as well as the other team members. I was on my own until I could find them again. There was no point trying to yell out to them - the noise of river and rain drowned out any voices.

We'd figured the river crossing was about an hour away from the gold site and so I determined to walk for an hour and then camp, hoping I'd find the track and the rest of my team by then. But it was not to be. By the time my hour was up, I knew I was hopelessly lost and needed to just stop and camp. The rain was showing signs of easing and by 3 pm it had almost entirely stopped. By 4 pm the clouds were dissipating and the afternoon sun was starting to shine through between cloud layers. I knew the river level would be up for another day or two as the rainfall in the mountains around fed its way down to the river. It's always like this in the highlands of PNG.

With the rain now stopped I had a chance to at least set up camp and remain dry. Clearing a little area where I could stretch out my waterproof sheet as a shelter, I soon discovered that every leaf, every branch, every tree had a thousand water droplets ready to fall onto me with the slightest shake! Finding some saplings nearby, I bent them over to snap, and made myself a rough frame on which to stretch the waterproof sheet. This would at least stop the drops falling on me, though the ground was still very wet to lie on, something I'd have to put up with. I gathered fern leaves to try and make a bush mattress. The noodles would have to wait, I didn't have a saucepan or pot to cook them - that was in the pack the boys were carrying. But at least some canned tuna put something into my tummy.

By about 5 pm I'd set up things for the night and just had to wait out the last hour or two of the afternoon before it got dark. I lay quietly under my shelter trying to get comfortable knowing that I'd be soaked by morning from the moisture in the ground.

Then I heard it. A rustling. There was something nearby, I could hear it. I tried to determine what direction the noise was coming from and turned to my left, rolling over as I did. Through the undergrowth I could see something moving around. It was black and so a little hard to see in the fading light. It was a bird! Yes, it was a Bird of Paradise.

I watched mesmerised as it seemed to clear a small area of leaves and twigs. What a beautiful treat I was being given, I thought, to see this rare bird in the wild.

But then the most amazing thing happened. My heart skipped a beat as the bird transformed into a ballerina. Its feathers suddenly flipped out so it looked like it had a skirt on. As it started hopping around in a little dance routine, it turned and faced me. The front of its breast was gleaming in the dying rays of sunlight beaming through the trees. It was brilliant green, then yellow and red as the colours of the rainbow glistened like a hologram. I could hardly take a breath, so amazing and beautiful was this bird's little courtship dance. It was the most beautiful thing I had ever seen and my heart was pounding with excitement.

For several minutes the little bird danced around, obviously trying to impress a prospective mate watching from the branches above me. I didn't see her but I didn't need to. I could not have been more impressed and know I would have instantly rushed into his nest with him if he was courting me! I felt like this display must have been just for me anyway.

All too soon it was over and the little bird disappeared. I lay frozen for sometime trying to absorb the beauty and majesty of what I had just witnessed. Then it dawned on me. This is the *nenge* bird, and this is what it is all about. Now I understand how sacred is this secret ritual it has now performed for me. Am I the first woman among the Moi people to witness it? Now I understand why they couldn't tell me about it. It's impossible to describe anyway, it is so beautiful.

I felt humbled by my previous attitude towards the *nenge* bird, my selfish pestering to Justin and the other elders to know more about it, as if I was the most important person in the world. I knew that seeing the bird now had changed me, but I couldn't describe how, I just knew something within me was different. I used to think that I was being left out of the experience of knowing it, but now I felt the privilege of being one of just a handful of Moi people to whom it had revealed itself. And I knew that this experience would carry responsibility; the responsibility of leadership.

My thoughts were racing as they explored different aspects of my encounter with the *nenge* bird. Lying on the damp ground as the darkness and cool of night enveloped me, shielded from the constant drops of rain dripping from the trees above me by a single sheet of waterproof cloth, open on all sides to the creatures of the night and lost to the rest of the world, I was totally at peace. Nothing mattered more to me than this meeting with *nenge*. I had been transfixed, transformed and translated to another planet. Surely this must be better even than getting married! I dared to think of the superlative nature of the last hour and how anything else must pale in comparison. And then I realised I was thinking of Justin again.

I couldn't wait to see him again and tell him of this. They were so right and I was so impatient. *Nenge* would reveal itself to me when it was ready, when the time was right, and now it had happened. They were so right to not tell me. Finally I understood why someone who had been told the story of such an encounter would never be able to achieve leadership in the tribe themselves, and why my grandfather was denied leadership because Justin's grandfather had unwittingly told him the story. Without first-hand experience, you cannot be touched personally by *nenge*. You cannot experience what goes on in your heart when *nenge* surprises you by revealing itself to you. You cannot know what it is like to be in a situation so desperate as an airplane accident or lost on the banks of a flooded river, yet to have an experience that so transcends the circumstances around you that they don't matter anymore, such is your peace and joy. And without that experience, you are not equipped for leadership.

Now I understood why the *nenge* bird was held in such awe and respect by the Moi people, especially the elders. This little bird was more than a mascot for the tribe. It was life itself. Without it, the core of Moiaimba culture was empty, and the tribe would collapse. I'd talked the talk of the importance of preserving the habitat of the *nenge* bird, which is right where the gold vein is, but realise I didn't understand it. But now I did and my commitment to protect its habitat had now become more than a cause. It had become a personal agenda, necessary to protect Moiaimba culture at its heart.

Another thought entered my mind. If it was because of the flash flood that I had met *nenge*, was it also protecting itself and its environment by using the flash flood to destroy those who will not protect it? The idea that the *nenge* bird could actually have that sort of power began to overwhelm me with gratefulness that I had been saved to meet it. And what about the perfect circumstances, as if they had been engineered? Here I am alone, without Justin. If I'd been with him, I would not have been alone or exactly in this place to meet the *nenge* bird. Once again I was taken into this new world of the *nenge* bird as I began to understand the power that it had.

It was dark by now and with eyes closed, oblivious to my surroundings, I slipped into a deep sleep. *Nenge* was watching over me, I had no fear of the night.

CHAPTER 19

THE RESCUE

The runner reached Mambusu after dark. One of the survivors of the Member's team, he'd run back to raise the alarm so that a search and rescue party could be sent out. The message he carried was grim. The surveyors had been washed away in the full force of the flash flood. The Member had been caught up in the water close to the river bank and was last seen struggling to keep his head above water as he was swirled downstream. Several others of his team had also suffered the same fate though he and another person had managed to get to higher ground and were safe.

Umbare David quickly heard about it and asked the messenger about Lily and her team's fate. The messenger knew nothing about them, or even that they were in the area as well. David knew full well that it could be several days before the river subsided enough to do a full search for those who were alive - and dead.

He decided to ring Justin.

"Hi there Uncle," said Justin, "you are calling very late in the night, what's going on?"

"Lupiano, there's been a development I need to inform you about. A survivor of a flash flood that has washed away some of the Member's survey team has returned. We don't know if the Member is safe or not. Apparently he was caught up in the waters on the edge of the river."

"Had Lily's team crossed the river already? Do we know anything about her whereabouts? Is she safe?" Justin suddenly had many questions and David could tell by his voice that he was now worried. After all, he had approved Lily going off by herself without him, and now he was helpless to do anything.

"No, we don't have any information about Lily," said David truthfully. "The messenger from the Member's group said they had not seen her or even knew she was in the area."

"I'm worried for her, David. But there is nothing I can really do except continue to worry! I think praying for her safety will help. What do you plan? Can you get a few men down there tomorrow to make sure she and the team are ok?"

"Lupiano, yes, that's our intention. I'll get in touch with you again as soon as we have any information to pass on. Meanwhile try not to worry too much, I'm sure she is ok. She is a smart girl you know, and the boys she is with know that country like the back of their hand. They wouldn't have let themselves get caught in a flash flood."

"I know you are right," replied Justin, "but there is the uncertainty, you know."

David quickly contacted the rest of the Foundation committee and they made plans to send a team to the area in the morning.

As dawn broke next day, it was clear that the storm clouds had passed and a gentle mist swept over the valley, blurring the line between tree top and cloud base. There was a beautiful freshness in the air and I could hear the birds of paradise singing in the distance. I couldn't believe that I had slept so soundly despite being in the damp coolness of the jungle. My heart was still singing as I recalled the events of the day before - the tragedy of the flash flood and the joy of meeting the *nenge* bird. It was not a dream for here I was, still in the jungle. I rolled a little to the left hoping to see the bird again but all I could see was undergrowth.

It was time to move on now, but where? How? I was lost and had no idea if I was upstream or downstream from the gold site. Still shrouded in the cocoon of morning fog, I couldn't even tell which direction was north. But still my heart was at peace. *Nenge* was here, walking beside me. I couldn't see it but I knew it was there. This *nenge* who can send the raging waters is the same one who stills my heart in the midst of the flood.

I decided to move out but always keep track of where I had slept last night. As I moved further and further away I hoped I would find the path again, or perhaps even find the rest of my team. So I started out in one direction, keeping as much of a straight line as I could, 50 steps. Nothing, so 50 steps back again from where I had come. Then another direction, 90 degrees to the first. 50 paces out and back. Each time I became a little more familiar with where I had slept. Broken twigs and branches on trees helped me find my way back. After all four directions around the compass points had found nothing familiar, I increased it to 100 paces in each direction. Then 200 paces, then 300. As I was about to turn back on one direction, I heard a sound. In the distance the sound of rushing water. I was near the river again.

Careful not to rush and lose my way again, I deliberately broke branches as I moved towards the sound. Suddenly I was confronted with a sight I had totally not expected. In amongst the trees was an aircraft, the one that Justin had crashed in a few months ago. My heart leapt. Nose down into the trees, it was covered in mould and moss and would soon be invisible in the jungle. When we had rescued Justin I hadn't paid any attention to the aircraft, in fact I didn't even see it. I had been too busy rescuing and caring for Justin, who had dragged himself down to the water's edge with a broken ankle.

Suddenly the incredible maze of what was happening to me was becoming apparent. I had seen the *nenge* in almost the same place as Justin had after he pulled himself from the wreckage and lay in the bush overnight, both of us in very unusual and distressing circumstances. And now we were sharing in an experience that was too amazing to even consider as coincidence.

I recalled the day we drew a map of where Justin had crashed. We marked the crash site and where we rescued him from at the river's edge, and then marked where the gold vein was. To our surprise, they were the same place! We could only conclude that *nenge* was the real gold of the Moi people. To mine the gold in the ground would destroy the habitat of the real gold that lives in the Moi people's hearts and minds.

As I made my way down to the river, I knew I was retracing Justin's steps as it were, as he dragged himself there. I don't know how he did it as I had to fight my way through the bush. But he was also pumped up after meeting *nenge*, and anything was possible.

The river was still in flood, just a mass of swirling brown water lapping up into the bush on the sides. I was happy. I knew where I was now. I would never forget the place where I found Justin. I also knew that I was at the gold site so the rest of the team must be close at hand. I would wait for them here. This was *nenge's* home and where I belonged now.

CHAPTER 20

THE VICTORY

The bodies of the three surveyors were never found. Lupo Warina was luckier. The rescue team found him on the river bank soon after they arrived at the scene, still with his boots on - exhausted but uninjured apart from a few minor scratches and bruises. It had been a humbling experience for him. The other members of his group also survived unscathed.

My survey group soon turned up at the gold site and found me waiting for them. We were able to complete the survey required though had to wait another day before the river subsided enough for us to cross and make our way home. By then our own rescue team was waiting for us on the other side of the river, glad to find that we had survived the flash flood.

I knew that Justin had to be the first one to know about my first-hand experience meeting the *nenge* bird. I didn't know if I could do that over the phone and so decided to wait until he returned from Sydney with his mother in a few days. I was struggling to contain my excitement but the distraction of wedding preparations would be good. The last few days had put me behind my schedule so I had a lot of catching up to do. First priority though was to prepare and submit the alluvial mining application using the survey information.

The women of Mambusu had gone out of their way to welcome me back. Word had spread quickly of the misadventure of the Member and his party and there was obvious concern for my welfare as well. But the relief when they got the news that my team and I were safe was palpable.

Deciding that they should welcome me as a group at the Guest Haus, the women had prepared a beautiful meal, ginger chicken and rice, *kaukau* with greens. Tired as I was from the long walk home again from the river, their presence gave me inspiration and motivation and I seemed to get a second wind of energy. I felt like I was being pampered as one of the women handed me a plate with what seemed like a mountain of food.

They asked about the trip and the events that had happened, especially the Member's misfortune, but I gave no hint as to my own wonderful meeting with the *nenge* bird. They would hear of it in time, but not now. Justin needed to be the first to hear, and from me, not community gossip.

Discussion drifted onto our wedding plans and the things they were doing in preparation. Everything seemed to be going well and it was obvious some had stepped in to take on extra things to help me. Then one of the wives raised the issue of their sabotage at the shed.

"I think we might have stopped our husbands going to the shed," she said, "mine has stayed home every night since, though he hasn't said anything about it to me yet."

A chorus of *"em nau"* and *"tru, tru"* went up as the others agreed, all with smiles on their faces!

"I don't think they realise who did it," said another.

"Let's keep it that way then," I said, "We don't want any of them getting upset about it and taking it out on us."

One of the women acted out closing her mouth as if it were a zipper, the others laughed.

"Seriously though," I continued, "I think we achieved what we set out to, and that was to stop your husbands going there."

CHAPTER 21

THE PAYMENT

Hendros Kipa was definitely not his usual self as he walked through Mambusu towards the Guest Haus. People had noticed that something was different. There had been a change, and his wife more than anyone noticed that change. His head was high, not proud, but confident, something he had not been for some time. She was the only one though who knew the reason for the change, and she felt proud that she'd been able to take a course of action to bring about that change. She actually felt like there was something exciting now happening in their relationship together. They'd shared an honesty together through this very difficult time and it had brought them closer. She realised she actually could help to bring about change by being smart and doing it in the right way.

The combined efforts of the women to sabotage the Ace Place were beginning to bear fruit, at least in her husband's life. He had been brought down to his knees, yet somehow, rather than being blackmailed by the Member, he was now being given the opportunity to start again. She knew he would not waste that opportunity.

It was three days after the Member had been rescued from the river and, while still feeling a little bruised from the experience, he was recovering well. After a short knock on the Guest Haus door, Hendros let himself in and saw the Member sitting in one of the old lounge chairs. The Member looked up and, inviting Hendros over to sit next to him in the adjacent chair, started to gloat. Hendros acknowledged his invitation but stayed standing.

"Ah, Hendros my brother, good to see you again," the Member said.

Hendros was not going to be pushed around in this conversation though and had decided that he'd call the shots this time.

"Member, what a surprise to see you here like this. Though I'm very glad that you were not washed away like your surveyors. I hope you are recovering ok?" he offered.

The Member noticed Hendros' confidence, which took him by surprise - he expected the man to come grovelling to him. After all, he had set him up to fail and there was no way he could repay the *dinau* unless he'd stolen the money from the Foundation.

"Member I'll come straight to the point of my visit - to pay off my *dinau*," said Hendros, looking the Member in the eye. He pulled out a grubby brown envelope from his pocket and handed it to the Member. "Here's the full amount of K8,000 as demanded."

The Member looked a little puzzled. He would not have expected the man to be so confident about the matter if he had stolen the money. In fact, he was handing it over in broad daylight where anyone could see the transaction taking place.

Opening the envelope, he pulled out the notes and counted them.

"Well, ah, I'm glad you could pay it back brother…" was all the Member could say.

"One more thing I need to say to you," continued Hendros, interrupting the Member. "You have influenced this community for too long with your gambling and drinking club which has pulled good men away from their families and caused financial hardship to many of them. Now that your scheme to blackmail us through our *dinaus* is out in the open, your business is no longer welcome here. You tried to chop down a tree to catch a *kuskus*, but the tree has fallen on you now and the *kuskus* is free. We'll see you at the voting booth."

Without even offering to shake the Member's hand, Hendros turned around and walked out of the Guest Haus door, leaving the Member with a deep frown on his face. How had Hendros managed to get the money to pay the *dinau*? But the biggest shock was that the Member now realised he had lost his power over Hendros, and probably most of the men in Mambusu.

It was then that he noticed it. In the shadow of curtains in the corner of the Mambusu Guest Haus lounge, a flicker of sunlight touched a wooden surface. He immediately recognised it as rosewood. He sat up in his lounge chair and stared at it. His eyes began to follow the line of the timber into the shadows, but he could see it clearly now. Familiar emblems were carved into it. Now he could see, it was a chair. The rosewood chair! His heart skipped a beat as he suddenly gulped for breath. It was exactly as the *tumbuna* legends described it. Slowly his eyes scanned up and then down the legs, then across the armrests and up the rattan backrest. It was indeed a remarkable carving, a solid piece carved from a single tree, something so exquisite and majestic, it could only be fit for a king.

The only parts that puzzled him were the carvings at the base of the armrest. They looked like a skirt or something, but he had no idea what they meant. He shouldn't have any idea. Only those who have seen the *nenge* know that they portray the *nenge* bird in its dance. No other proof that he was not the true leader of the Moi people was needed.

Lupo slumped back in his lounge chair, exhaustion from both his ordeal at the river and with Hendros, and now seeing the chair, overtook him and he closed his eyes. Now the reality of Lily's words began to sink in. Justin was Lupiano. Now he, Lupo Warina, was the pretender to the throne.

CHAPTER 22

THE EVICTION

It was a normal hot and steamy coastal day a few days later when I drove to Jackson's International Airport to meet Justin, who was arriving on the mid afternoon flight from Sydney, via Brisbane. Winding around the streets of 6 Mile were the familiar sights of the crowds of people in the market place, dust and rubbish littering the roadside, and children competing for their mother's attention over *bilums* of market produce slung from their foreheads. Market benches and floor space around them were covered with produce of all kinds, from peanuts, coconuts and *karuka* nuts to pumpkin tips and various other *kumu* leaves, while sweet potato, taro, yams and English potatoes competed with tomatoes, pumpkins, corn and the occasional lemon. All laid out on tatty old rice bags.

The kaleidoscope of colour was beautiful. The smell was not, the fresh vegetable aromas overpowered by the stench of dirty drains that weaved around and through the market precinct. The noise of sellers raising their voice to be heard clearly by buyers browsing by could be heard through my open car window.

"Two kina, two kina, two kina for six…" It reminded me of how fortunate we were at Mambusu, where market prices were a fraction the cost - especially when *wantoks* often gave you a further discount.

After submitting the alluvial mining application, I'd decided to call in to see some relatives living in the Mambusu settlement at 9 Mile before doubling back to the airport at 7 Mile. While the road was the main one leading north east out of Moresby and into the mountain ranges which enclosed the famous Kokoda Trail, it was still only a one lane road, constructed, it seemed, of potholes covered with bitumen. The last section was just dirt road - potholes not covered with bitumen. Shanty houses were popping up all over any section of land that appeared vacant. These squatters would soon discover who the land owner was and would invariably be asked to pay a fee for the privilege of living there. Within a day or two another visitor, also claiming to be the landowner, would visit and demand their fee. And so it would go on.

The names of senior politicians would sometimes be thrown around in the conversation with the settlers, just so they were aware of the authority the visitors carried to seek compensation for their privilege. For those who were able to wade through this onslaught of debtors, the uncertainty certainly meant few were interested in building anything out of permanent materials. So more and more temporary houses began to spring up, littering the landscape with specks of blue tarpaulin, plastic sheets and discarded roofing iron.

Basic services in these communities were non-existent - rubbish accumulated on the streets, sometimes in piles on street corners; erosion caused drains and ditches to form where ever the rain dictated; and raw sewerage flowed freely in the drains. Just as the Member had found a few months earlier, I had to pick my way carefully between the houses to reach my *wantok's* place.

"Ayo, so nice to see you," my cousins Manny and Eric greeted me, with Manny throwing her arms around me.

"Yeah, so nice for me too to see you again," I replied, still embraced by Manny.

"Eh, yu wanem kain meri na yu kam long dispela ples nogut?" Manny asked quite assertively, almost arrogantly. The question had the connotation that somehow I had now risen above settlement status on the social ladder. But that was far from the truth as far as I was concerned. These were my people. I couldn't tell them about meeting the *nenge* bird, but I realised I was feeling the responsibility of leadership much more than I did before.

Manny noticed that I didn't answer her, and interrupted herself. "I'll go and make a cup of tea, you ready for one?" she said.

"I sure am," I replied, "I just spent three hours in a government department so need it!" The conversation continued in Tok Pisin.

"So what brings you here? It must be two or three years since we last saw you, and that was when we came back to Mambusu for the *haus krai*," Eric asked.

"Oh, you know, I had a bit of time to kill while here in POM so wanted to catch up with you."

"So what's this we hear about you getting married soon, eh?" Manny couldn't help but know the latest gossip.

"That's right, Justin and I are getting married in a few weeks. You guys are welcome to come and join us. The *mumu* will be the biggest ever at Mambusu!"

"I hear your Justin might be standing for election?" Eric chipped in.

"Yeah, some friends have encouraged him to do that but I am not sure what he is thinking at the moment. There are some good reasons why he is suitable. He meets the cultural requirements for leadership, in fact he is Lupiano," I replied.

"I thought that stuff was part of our old traditions but long since gone. I mean Lupo Warina doesn't meet some of those requirements but he is still our parliamentary member," said Eric.

"Well, to cut a long story short," I said, "Justin's mother was the small girl who was taken out of the village and to Australia by her father, the gold miner…"

"Yeah, we all know that story," chipped in Manny.

"So Justin meets all the requirements to be Lupiano," I said.

"Well we need someone to be our Member who is not always trying to take advantage of us," said Manny. "This latest rumour is making a lot of people pretty anxious here."

"What latest rumour? Tell me about it," I said.

"Oh, I thought you'd know about it," said Manny, "you know, that the settlement is going to be evicted so that a bunch of politicians can build expensive housing. It will force us all to find somewhere else to live even though we've lived here for ten years now."

"No, I hadn't heard," I replied. "That doesn't sound good. What else do you know?"

"It's hard to find out all the details but my uncle who works at Parliament House is trying to find out more. It seems like a group of political leaders have got a pact to get rich by building houses here. Apparently they've been able to gain leases for the land." Eric looked concerned as he spoke.

"It's just not fair," said Manny, "every time we try and apply for a lease, it is always more money than we can afford, and then there are the bribes we are expected to pay the government workers."

Eric continued. "The Post Courier had an article last week which alerted us to the scheme. Of course it was written in a way which made it look like it was going to be a huge benefit for the community. But we could read between the lines - the only way it could go ahead would be if we were evicted."

"I'm sorry to hear that this is happening," I said. "Was there any indication of who is behind it?"

"No, it only referred to 'leaders' but no names. However our own MP has had a couple of visits here in the last six months. He walked around the settlement and looked like he had a couple of surveyors with him. He seemed very interested in taking measurements."

"Yeah, it was obvious he was trying to *gris* people to get their vote and gave away some K5 notes, but then was a bit distracted with his survey. Made his efforts with people look a bit *giaman!*" said Manny.

"That's very interesting then," I said, "the Member wanting votes but possibly involved in evicting the settlement. Justin will be very interested to hear of this. I guess we'll have to find out more somehow."

Already I was thinking of how we could get a clear picture of what was happening but it had already struck me that exposing this might provide the most crucial opportunity to rob the Member of votes at the election. The people of Mambusu are not going to vote for someone preparing to evict them!

Checking my watch I realised time had flown and I needed to get out to the airport. With a quick swig to drain the last vestiges of tea from my host's enamel mug, I bade them farewell.

"Make sure you let us know what's happening," called out Manny as she watched me straddle the drain.

"Maybe I'll bring Justin, I mean Lupiano, with me next time as well," I yelled with a big smile.

Ok Mr Warina, I thought, game on!!

CHAPTER 23

THE MATRIARCH

I watched Justin and his mother as they came into the International Terminal after clearing customs. I must admit my heart leapt a little when he first appeared. I'd missed him! Then his mother appeared. I started to cry. The significance of her coming back was huge but no more so than for her. She had no memory of her infancy in PNG. Yet here she was; the Matriarch of Mambusu had finally returned home.

I'd wondered what she would look like. But she was beautiful beyond description and looked totally as if she belonged here. Her light brown skin shined, and her wavy hair, now white, looked so elegant. I was immediately mesmerised by the beauty of this woman who was, I reminded myself, of the same blood as me. She looked old but still seemed young; she was mature but still had a twinkle of youthful mischief in her eyes; even in the midst of totally new and unfamiliar surroundings she still looked calm and poised. I knew straight away that I couldn't help but love her.

I couldn't help myself and rushed up to her and wrapped

my arms around her. I felt her tears on my shoulder as we embraced. We didn't need to say anything. Finally I released her and swung around to embrace Justin, whose face beamed. This was such a proud moment for him too.

We collected our bags and headed for the car. I was too overcome with emotion to say much but once we found the car, the conversation began to flow. There was so much to catch up on. The thing of course that never moved from being at the front of my mind though was being able to tell him about meeting the *nenge* bird. But for the immediate I was engrossed in getting to know my future mother-in-law.

I sat in the back seat next to her while Justin drove. No sooner had we fastened our seat belts than she took hold of my hand. I was going to tell her all about Moresby as we drove to the hotel but before I could say anything, she spoke.

"Oh Lily dear, this is such a wonderful dream come true for me. I have prayed for Justin for all these years and now my prayers have been answered. He's told me all about you and I am so absolutely delighted that he has found you. I am so looking forward to getting to know you better." She squeezed my hand, and kept holding it.

I was speechless but in my heart I was full of praise for this wonderful woman who was now gracing my life.

We'd settled mother into her hotel room and, finally, I thought I could tell Justin what had happened now that we were alone again.

"I've got so much to tell you," I said to him, "so much has happened since you've been away."

"Well I am so thankful that you were not injured in the flash flood," he said. I could see it in his eyes. What I didn't realise was that he could see something in my eyes. "How is the Member? I was sorry to hear that he lost some of his surveyors."

"Yes, that was so sad. Mr Warina is recovering but he'll be ok, more a scare and emotional damage to his ego than physical hurt," I replied.

"Has he been up to any more tricks that you know of?"

"Well, interesting you should ask," I said, "because I visited Manny and Eric at Mambusu 9 Mile settlement just before I picked you up. They say there is a move on by a group of politicians to evict the settlement and build some housing units. We don't know if Lupo is part of it yet but we need to find out quickly."

"That would be very interesting indeed. If the settlement community found out he was involved, they would be certain not to vote for him!" responded Justin.

"Yep, and I was able to lodge the application for an alluvial gold licence today as well, so we are moving ahead on that ok."

"I guess that Lupo never completed his survey after the flash flood so looks like we got in before he did," said Justin.

"It was going to be so close, you know, both of us out there trying to survey and get our application in first." As I said this, a thought came to my mind. "Why do you think that flash flood happened right at that exact moment? His surveyors were right in the middle of the river and had no hope of escaping."

Justin thought for a moment and said, "You know I've been thinking about that too. There are too many coincidences here. But I feel like the *nenge* bird was somehow behind it all, almost like it didn't want Lupo to succeed but did want you to succeed."

"That's exactly what I was thinking too. Isn't that strange, like this bird is still in control of its area. The area we were surveying was both the gold seam and the bird's habitat."

I could see the conversation now leading me to tell Justin. I was excited and yet a bit apprehensive. How would he react?

"Lily," he said, "can you describe to me the carvings on my grandfather's chair?"

That's a strange question, I thought, but continued with my reply.

"Yes, that's easy, how many times have I studied it? There is a crocodile wrapped around by a snake on the armrests, the feet look like dog's feet, the back seems to have a tribal mask engraved into it," I paused, "and then there is the bird of paradise dancing at the top of the front legs."

"I knew it," shouted Justin excitedly, "I knew you'd seen the *nenge* bird!" He jumped up and wrapped his arms around me giving me the biggest squeeze.

"How did you know?" I shot back at him.

"Something was different about you the moment I saw you at the airport and I knew it had to be *nenge*. You've got a confidence and assurance that you never had before," he said.

"I never realised that, I just wanted you to know so badly. But you did... you did know!"

"That's what meeting the *nenge* bird does to you, or should I say it's what the bird does to you. Now you understand why you can't have a fake experience with it, you have to see it yourself," Justin explained.

"I am so glad you and the elders held your ground and didn't give in and tell me about it. It was the most beautiful experience, lying lost on the jungle floor, and then all of a sudden it's there performing its beautiful dance. Suddenly all my fear was taken away. It was amazing."

"These are the lessons of leadership that can't come second -hand. Once you've met the *nenge,* it touches something deep inside you and gives you the confidence to move forward without fear."

"I'm so excited," I said, "because now we can move ahead in leading our community together, both now meeting the cultural leadership requirements." After a pause I continued. "You know, I think that we are the only people in this generation who have seen the *nenge.* Uncle David and the others are a past generation. I wonder how long before *nenge* will need to appoint a new generation of leadership?"

"Lily there is now something very important we need to decide on," said Justin.

"I know, I've been thinking lots about it since you left," I replied.

"Well that's really good because this will be something which is very important to our community," said Justin.

"I'm so glad you feel that way too," I replied, "It is so important that we invite the right people to our wedding and don't have anyone feeling left out. I know it may cost more for catering, but I'm so glad you feel the same way." I reached up and gave Justin a squeeze around the waist, kind of a half hug.

He paused for a moment and I thought he took a deep breath before replying to me. "Actually I wasn't thinking of the wedding. I was thinking about whether I stand for elections or not."

I wanted to hit him! Isn't this typical of men, always on a different track than us? But he was right, that was the most important decision we had to make now.

"I think we need to discover if Mr Warina is involved in the eviction plans at the settlement first," I said, though in my heart I knew that we were both now destined for leadership roles.

CHAPTER 24

THE GOLDEN FUTURE

The Leadership Tribunal predictably ruled against Mr Warina and he was ousted from parliament and his position as Member for Moi for the remaining duration of the term. The Electoral Commission decided that rather than have a by-election so close to the date set for elections, the seat would remain vacant. However there was no ruling beyond the current term of office and so Mr Warina was cleared to stand again as the Member for Moi if he so desired.

Lupo Warina had been thinking over plans for re-election and what direction his campaign would take. With his discovery of the rosewood chair, and confirmation now that Justin was indeed Lupiano, he knew that it would be a battle if Justin decided to stand also. So far he had heard nothing that would confirm that Justin was to stand, though some of the local people were expressing support for him if he did. Warina knew that he would have to have a strong policy case which very clearly demonstrated his leadership over Justin. He played around with some slogans which would be at the forefront of his campaign advertising and get people's attention. He seemed to be favouring one that went something like this:

Warina for a Golden Future.

That kept his name in focus while dangling the carrot of gold in front of his constituents. Mining that gold would be the key. Then another thought came to him. He could undermine any campaign by Justin by focusing on the future - society has moved on and the old ways and stories no longer have relevance to the modern age. Justin will no doubt focus people back on who he is because of his history. But Lupo will focus people on the future and all that awaits them there. If you vote for Justin, you are voting for the past - if you vote for Warina you are voting for the future! That's it, he thought.

His platform would be based around establishing a mine, as he had already tried to do but which failed when people became nervous about possible corruption on his part. So he would find another consortium he could work with. Clearly spelling out the benefits to the community that would come with a mine was paramount. Things like school buildings, water supply, training for school leavers, jobs for the community, more housing, aid posts in the area.... all the benefits which normally are promised by mining companies.

This would be great for the local Moi area 'village' community but there was a second electoral group which also needed his attention, and that was the growing number of people who resided in Port Moresby, particularly in the 'Mambusu' settlement near 9 Mile. Many of these people were smarter than those in the village community, mainly because of their exposure to city life. They had learned politics and a number, more than in the village community, were educated and working. So finding a way to ensure their support in the upcoming election was a fresh challenge for him.

At least he was sure of one thing. Justin Lupiano had had no contact with the settlement community, most would hardly know of him, so he, Lupo Warina, had a distinct advantage over Justin. He would need to act assertively, even aggressively, to maintain that advantage. So plans were made for him to hold a rally in 9 Mile.

A few days later Lupo Warina found himself walking along the muddy road into the Mambusu settlement at 9 Mile. This was to be an introductory visit with a few faithful supporters and relatives. Some of them met him at the turn off to the settlement and walked in with him. The fact of his dismissal from office hardly seemed to matter, in fact they saw it as victimisation, that he had been targeted politically by his adversaries.

Warina had prepared for this visit. His pockets were stashed once more with 10 kina notes, ready to hand out to any constituent who had a need for it. But he would wait for a while before handing any out. That way he could keep his friends close at hand, dangling the carrot of a 10 kina note to keep their attention.

He was also well aware of the needs of these settlement friends, so he could target his campaign speeches to highlight improvements in the matters which affected settlements most.

The group arrived at a small community hall hidden away in the settlement. Some cans of Coke and Fanta, warmed in the tropical heat, were ready waiting for them, supplied by some of the settlement women, wives of the supporters. They sat down on dilapidated but functional chairs around a scratched wooden table and Warina introduced the meeting.

"Ladies and Gentlemen, thank you for being available today. You know the reason for this meeting as well as I do. I want to kick off my re-election campaign soon and so would like to do that here in Mambusu settlement. So many people from our Moi electorate have come to live here over the years, and I know you have been neglected in so many ways. So I want to recognise your situation and focus on a future with bright outcomes for you here." Warina paused for a few seconds to allow the significance of future blessings through him to register.

"We'll be going ahead with the gold mine back home and there will be huge benefits for our community from that. I want to make sure that our people here in Port Moresby also benefit. Under me, I will ensure that development comes to 9 Mile settlement. It's what I am calling a golden future. So I want to introduce you to my slogan for this upcoming election: Warina for a Golden Future."

He looked around at the group of 10 or 12 who had joined him and acknowledged their smiles and nods of approval. He would now change his tone and make his discussion more inclusive of his friends - it was now 'we' and not 'I' who would win this election.

"The most important thing now," he continued, "if we are to win this upcoming election, is that we have a good strong, dedicated team who can work to ensure that every settlement dweller knows about their future under me. You are the beginning of that team."

He reached into his pocket and pulled out a wad of 10 kina notes, placing it on the table in front of him. Eyes eager to distribute the notes stared at the wad. Warina knew he now had their full attention.

"First of all, funding for our campaign is not an issue. So I'd like to hand out some funds to enable you to get started and not be out of pocket," he said. What he really meant was that he would pay for their allegiance, knowing full well that his money would probably be spent on beer anyway.

In unison the group moved noticeably closer to the table, hands poised ready to receive their portion of campaign funds. Warina carefully and deliberately opened the pack and started handing round the K10 notes like he was dealing a pack of cards. Each person received four or five notes before the wad ran out. There were more smiling faces and nodding heads.

"Member, what's your strategy now then?" asked one of the men as he shuffled the notes in his hands.

"Well, we need to have a very visible presence in the settlement," replied Warina. "What do you think about the idea of using my slogan, 'Warina for a Golden Future'?"

"That's a great idea, and a great slogan, Member," another man responded, eager to be seen to stand with the now former Member. "Perhaps we could have some posters made with your photo and we can stick them up on houses all through the settlement?"

"Now that's a great idea my brother, in fact I'll head down to the print shop after this meeting to arrange the posters. Getting my face and slogan visible in every corner of the settlement will be a great start."

The group were starting to warm up and over the next hour many suggestions were made of ways to improve the campaign, some good, some not so good. Warina was relieved to see how easy it had been to engage this group and get them working constructively in his campaign.

One of the suggestions he really liked, and that was to give every settlement family a 10kg bag of rice with the words, 'Donated by Lupo Warina - Warina for a Golden Future' printed or stamped on the rice bag. That would get his name and generosity into every house and woman's heart.

No one asked him about the Post Courier article, or about rumours of eviction, which pleased Warina very much. He was not ready to face that sort of scrutiny before his campaign had even commenced. Whatever any of them had heard about the rumours, he knew he now had a small team of dedicated volunteers who would advance his campaign in the settlement.

The meeting ended well, everyone very happy to be involved and happy to receive a bonus K10 as a personal gift from Warina as they prepared to walk back out through the settlement.

CHAPTER 25

THE DIARY

We drove back to Mambusu with Justin's mother the next day. I could tell that she was loving being back in PNG, even though she remembered nothing of her infancy here. But her eyes were alive as they sought to take in everything around her.

There was of course a big welcoming for our arrival at Mambusu. The community had been waiting to see again this long lost daughter of theirs. As we drove up towards the Guest Haus, a group of dancers in their traditional attire came towards the vehicle then split up to dance with one row on each side. Grass skirts swayed to the rhythm of the *kundu* drum beat; bare feet stepped delicately to the right then left then to the front, then back; ornamental shells clicked together around necklaces; feathers and leaves swayed from headdresses as their heads moved in time with the beat. This was a time of great joy and celebration.

When we finally made our way through the crowd and stopped in the gravelled Guest Haus car park, the crowd continued to gather round. Some had tears in their eyes, such was their joy. Everyone wanted to get a glimpse of mother. Justin opened the car door for her and, as she stepped out to put her feet once more on Moi soil, the older women came forward to embrace her, showering her with bouquets of local flowers. I saw most of the women from our fellowship come forward to welcome her. The next half hour was spent shaking hands - no one wanted to miss out on this event, one which would certainly add a new chapter into Moi folklore.

The next few days would be consumed by visits from the local community as the word spread out to all the distant villages that mother, the girl in the legend, had returned. But for now, she was exhausted after the drive to Mambusu and her flight the previous day, though would not admit it! Justin insisted though that she put her feet up for a rest and she grudgingly obliged.

I longed to find out from her all about her life, and how it was that she knew about her history. I knew I would have to wait until all the current commotion had passed and all the village people who wanted to meet her had had their chance. The opportunity to spend some time with her came two days later. I'd joined Justin and mother in the Guest Haus for breakfast and with no one now knocking at the front door, we knew we could enjoy some privacy.

"I'm so looking forward to hearing all about your life, Mama," I said. "I have so many questions, I don't know where to start!"

"Well my dear," replied mother, "why don't we start at the beginning. I know that my mother was from here, but why don't you tell me what you know about this because you have a whole side of the story that I would like to hear as well. You know, I only have the story that my father told me, and that wasn't much, except to say that my real mother was from PNG and died while giving birth to me."

"I've just realised something Mum," Justin interrupted. "I've just realised that the grandmother I knew was not your birth mother."

"That's right son, the mother I grew up with was the woman that your grandfather married after he returned from PNG. She was a wonderful lady and accepted me as if I was her own daughter. She is the birth mother of my brothers and sisters, your uncles and aunties."

"So how did you find out that your mother was from PNG?" I asked.

"Well, as a young girl growing up, my father never hid that from me. He would often talk about my mother, Leelak. He loved her so much. As he would describe her beautiful brown skin and brown eyes to me, he would explain to me that was why my skin was also brown and my hair dark and wavy. I was different to most of the Aussies around me. He knew that people may make a comment to me about my darker skin and he wanted me to be proud of who I was, of my heritage."

"So how come that I never heard anything about your mother as I grew up?" asked Justin.

"Your grandfather married his second wife when I was four years old. I guess we just got on with life after that. My brothers and sisters were born and we were just a happy big family." Mother paused to think for a few moments. "I guess by the time I married your father, that was all past history and none of it really seemed relevant any more. So it never got talked about."

I could tell that Justin was feeling the same sense of pain that I was feeling. That something so precious had been relegated to being of no value. That's probably why we felt it was so good that mother could return to Mambusu and really discover her roots.

She looked up at both of us and with a smile on her face said, "So tell me the story as you know it."

A look of shock suddenly enveloped Justin's face.

"What's the matter Justin?" I asked.

Justin looked at his mother. "Mum, did you know that grandfather wrote a diary about his time here?" The realisation had come to him that he had never mentioned the diary to his mother.

Mother's face squeezed into a look of disbelief.

"A diary?" she asked.

"Yes, grandfather wrote a diary about his time here. Have you never seen it?" replied Justin.

"A diary? No, I didn't know he had one. How strange, he never mentioned it at all."

"Well I found it in the seat of his rosewood chair. You remember when I started to renovate it last time I was back in Sydney?" said Justin.

"Yes, I do, the chair was in disrepair and you've done such a good job of fixing it up. It's so nice to see it here now. But why would a diary be hidden there?" she asked.

"I can't answer that Mum, it was hidden in the seat lining and I discovered it when reupholstering the seat cover. But it helps explain why you knew so little about your past, because grandfather wanted it that way. He wanted you to remember you mother but not be caught up in all the other drama of his visit here."

"But why would he do that?" asked mother.

"Well," replied Justin, "I suspect that he wanted you to know of your heritage but be able to feel fully part of the Australian society which you grew up in. I think he did it to protect you. At the same time, he wanted me to discover the diary so that I could fulfil my destiny, which is back here in Mambusu."

"Oh, there's so much I still don't understand. So tell me about this diary. Where is it now?" asked mother.

I excused myself for a few moments and fetched the diary from my room, then held it out to her with both hands.

At first she just stared at it, saying nothing. After a few minutes she reached out and gently took it from me, holding it tenderly.

It was just a tattered old book. But yet so much more. Within these pages the mystery of her birth would be revealed. A connection now between her father who she loved so much and who had loved her so much was once again made. Tears welled up in her eyes. We realised that she was ready to discover things she could only have wondered about, her very origins. This was indeed a sacred moment for her and Justin and I just watched as she began to consider all that this book might contain for her.

"There are two stories, Mum. One is what you have in your hands there, Grandfather's own recording of events and his thoughts and feelings. The other story is the local legends of those who were here when grandfather was. Lily is a distant relative of Leelak, in fact that why she is called Lily, and she and the elders will tell you their story."

Mother looked up at us both, cheeks now dripping with tears, and smiled. It was not a smile of sudden happiness. It was a smile of deep inner joy, the joy of finding something which has been hidden as a mystery for a lifetime, something that means she can at last know who she really is.

"I don't know what to say," she said, slowly opening up the pages. "His handwriting, it's so beautiful." Memories of her father flooded back.

"Mum, take it and read it, and we'll tell you the local legends when you are ready," said Justin.

How strange it was to think that mother was now able to discover her past directly from her father, through his own words written in the diary. This trip for her was going to be far more than just to attend our wedding!

Over the next few days mother would read the diary and come back to us with questions, and then hear the stories from the Moiaimba people's perspective.

This was the story that had led Justin to discover his own heritage and destiny to become the headman of the Moiaimba people. In his own words, his grandfather described how he came into Moi country seeking gold back in the 1920s and fell in love with Leelak, a local village girl. In due time they married and she bore a daughter - Justin's mother. But following Leelak's untimely death during childbirth, his grandfather had returned to Australia with his young daughter, who was never heard of again. Now that daughter had returned.

CHAPTER 26

THE VOW

With Justin home again, we could move ahead with preparations for our wedding. The women's group had been busy the whole time with their preparations, including planning for the food we'd need for a big group of people. We expected most if not all of the people in Mambusu would want to attend, and probably many from outlying villages. It was at times like these that people's generosity became so clear. Several local leaders had donated pigs for the feast, and a storehouse was filling up with sweet potato, yams, taro and other root vegetables as people contributed from their gardens.

Justin's mother was a huge help as she became a magnet for the local women who came to visit her and meet her. Though she had never learnt any of the Moiaimba language, leaving the area well before she could talk, she began to pick up some of it as the women taught her different words and phrases. Her intonation was perfect and shrieks of delight could often be heard from any group of women around her as she learnt new words. We marvelled at how at peace she was, and how much she had found her place here as well. Unfortunately it would not last as she would need to return to Australia in a few weeks.

But she would be immortalised in Moiaimba culture. As I listened I began to hear a term which I had not heard for many years. The women were referring to her by this name, *nenge nematanu moibe,* "mother of the people of the bird", shortened to *nenge-be.* It was a term of such endearment that it was the highest honour for a woman to receive.

I must admit the couple of weeks leading up to the wedding ceremony were a blur with so many preparations that kept us busy well into each evening. But finally the day arrived. This was a dream that I could never have imagined even a few months ago, before Justin turned up at the Mambusu Guest Haus one day and my life and that of our community changed forever.

Just as the tribal elders relaxed the cultural requirements for Justin's grandfather when he married Leelak, so they relaxed the requirements for Justin. I remembered back to when Uncle Umbare David first told us that the elders had chosen me to be Justin, or headman Lupiano's, wife.

With such a serious face he'd later said Justin would need to spend three months in the bush with only a bow and arrow, yes, naked, and if he survived, then we could marry. Justin hadn't known what to say, until Uncle David burst into laughter. So did we at the thought of it!

Last night Uncle David had visited the Guest Haus again to talk with us.

"Justin," he said, "I hope in time that you and your mother, *nenge-be,* will realise how significant this event is in the history of the Moiaimba tribe. We have fully recognised your heritage as *Lupiano*, our headman. Now to have *nenge-be* return and be among us is the fulfilment of all the stories that have been handed down to us since the 1920s. We didn't record our history in a book because our people didn't know how to read and write then. But when we write it down now for future generations, we will know that our stories were the truth and we can trust them."

Uncle David paused and looked at me.

"Daughter, you are going to formally marry Justin tomorrow. We know that by doing so, there is a breaking of the curse that his grandfather invoked upon Seri, your grandfather, because he told him about seeing the *nenge* bird. As both of you, as their grandchildren, enter into a new covenant relationship tomorrow, it ends the curse. Not only was Seri prohibited from becoming a leader among our people, but the extent to which that curse has flowed through to you as well has now been broken. You, as his granddaughter, will no longer come under that curse."

Justin had told me this before but I had forgotten it. I began to think about what it meant for me to also have seen the *nenge* bird first hand.

David continued. "The fact that the *nenge* bird revealed itself to you, Lily, is really significant for us. First of all it means you are now *nenge nematanu*, and as such, as you know, you are now regarded as a leader in our tribe. So tomorrow as you and Justin marry, we will honour you both as leaders in your own right, both called by *nenge*. This is the first time in our history that we have recognised both partners as *nenge nematanu*.

"There is one more matter of significance also. You know our culture is matrilineal, as our ancestors were when they came from islands for away. So we already enshrine the power of women in our society especially in matters such as land distribution and marriage. It was the women who saw that you were destined to marry Justin. But you are the first woman to see the *nenge* bird and so receive the title of *nenge nematanu.*

"We are living in an age where we are recognising that women can have a more active role in society and stand side by side with men in many ways. Your marriage relationship will provide us with a new vision of this, as you work side by side as leaders and bring a leadership which fully considers the men and the women in our society. The *nenge* bird has made this very clear to us by revealing itself to you, Lily."

I was beginning to realise that my sighting of the *nenge* was far more than just the realisation of my own personal desire to see it. I felt embarrassed now about all my pestering to want to see it without realising its greater significance. It was in fact signalling the start of a new era in leadership for the Moiaimba people, one that now recognised the need for women to take on more responsibility, while men allowed room for a greater sharing of responsibility. It was not about women taking over, it was about seeing that all of society was engaged in leadership. I felt the huge responsibility I now recognised was being placed upon me for the future with Justin.

These thoughts were running through my mind as I entered the church building, with Uncle David escorting me in place of my father. We'd decided on a western style Christian wedding ceremony in the Mambusu church building, followed by a Moiaimba style cultural ceremony and feast. Justin's mother had been wonderful because of her experience as a seamstress and had made a beautiful white full length wedding dress for me, using material she had brought with her from Sydney, a surprise for me! Justin had also bought a new, tailored, Anthony Squires suit while in Sydney. As my eyes set on his as he waited at the front of the church, I felt so proud to be marrying this absolutely handsome man.

Throughout the short ceremony where we committed ourselves to God and each other, I could hear the *kundu* drums beating in the distance as groups of dancers prepared for the feast. This was going to be a big party!

Justin had wanted to make sure that we were together in heart and mind as we married, and so we had spent time talking over what we knew about and expected of marriage. I was looking for something beyond just a traditional PNG view of marriage which sees the wife as subservient to her husband. Justin saw it very much as a partnership but recognised that, in the past, Moiaimba cultural expectations had meant that a wife was sometimes seen as just someone to have kids and work the gardens, and cement inter-clan relationships. But he saw it differently and wanted to make sure I also understood that.

He explained that he saw men and women created by God and both equally able to enter into a relationship with God based on the forgiveness of their sins that God offers. So we have an identity as God's children and the sin that destroys our self-esteem no longer has power over us.

Anyway, Justin explained that he saw marriage as a three-way relationship between a man and a woman and God, who treats the man and woman as equals. He said that problems in marriage happen when each partner has unfulfilled expectations of the other. That is mainly because our expectations are selfish. So we want the other person to meet our needs, and when they fail, disappointment results.

So arguments start and people drift apart. But when each partner is looking to God to meet their deep inner needs like self-esteem and identity, then they are able to reach out to the other partner in true love because it is no longer selfish.

It took me a while to understand what Justin was saying but when I thought back to how he accepted me and reached out to me when I told him I had been assaulted, and I expected him to reject me, I started to see the truth in what he was saying. His identity was grounded in the Creator God who accepts and forgives us when we have failings, and so he could offer that same acceptance and forgiveness to me.

At the same time Justin recognised that there are roles for both the man and the woman in a marriage, and the extension of this was that he saw each partner empowering the other in their separate roles, not conflicting or acting in jealousy. So I knew when the time came, he would be there to support me in every way he could. And I would willingly support him in any way I could when he had needs that I could meet.

So we had written our marriage vows together to express what we had talked about. This was my vow:

Justin Lupiano Orlando, On this our Wedding Day, I promise before God to love you with a love that reflects the love that God has shown me. I will accept you as you are, I will forgive you for your failings, but I will not let you remain in them. I will seek at all times to honour you and support you as my husband, and I will look to God first, together with you, to meet my needs.

Justin had a similar vow to me. It was a moving time for us as we shared in this moment of promise together. I knew we would be tested and there would be times when it would be hard to forgive, hard to accept situations, hard to offer him my total support, but I prayed they would be few and far between and we would have the grace to move beyond them quickly.

All too quickly the ceremony was over and we walked hand in hand out of the church and into the sunlight as a married couple. Rows of dancers now lined the pathway to the feast and quickly the *kundu* drums started beating and the dancers began their swaying in time to the beat.

Girls came forward and draped handmade flower *leis* over our heads while others threw other greenery such as leaves, flowers and cuttings over us. The aroma of *mumu* pig began to fill our noses as the stones and banana leaves were removed from the top of the earth ovens. A dozen large pigs and fifty chickens had been sacrificed for this party! Dancers were singing as they swirled around us, their songs telling the story.

Lupiano, hidden from us, now revealed,
Lupiano, hidden from us, now we see him;
Nenge-be, hidden from us, lost forever,
Nenge-be, hidden from us, now among us,
Lily, waiting for her husband, waiting for *nenge*,
Lily, now with her husband, now with *nenge*...

One of the first visitors to congratulate us were Kila and his wife, Konio, with their children.

"Hey, Auntie Lily," the eldest called out to me. "Now we can come and stay with you and Uncle Justin."

"Oooh, not so fast," his father responded quickly, "give them time to settle in .... congratulations to you both, this is such a magnificent time to be with you here in Mambusu. I am so happy to see you both finally married!"

Justin's continued single status had been a point of humour for Kila on many occasions!

"Hi Kila and Konio, so good to see you here as a family. Did you contribute a couple of the pigs?" Justin asked him with a grin.

"Oh no, unfortunately I had to hand them back," he replied with a reluctant sigh. "However, I've got some more news on Warina's involvement in the settlement eviction report which will definitely affect Mambusu settlement at 9 Mile. But we'll have plenty of time to talk that over tomorrow after the party."

"You are right, Kila," replied Justin. "Today I'm going to put all that aside and just enjoy being totally focused on my beautiful bride. Though I do have one announcement to make so keep your ears tuned in."

Kila put both hands up to his ears as if waiting to hear. But Justin would not give anything away, even to Kila.

A long table had been set up with chairs for ourselves and important visitors. Pig carcasses were being cut up and divided out onto plates. The most important parts of the pig were relegated to the most important visitors including Kila and Konio. Plates for food were handed out, until they ran out and banana leaves were substituted. Everyone would get a decent meal. Pig, chicken, and all sorts of root vegetable and greens draped over plates were being distributed as families and friends sat round on the grass around the Mambusu Guest Haus.

All too soon it was time for speeches. Most people had finished their meal, or were taking left overs back to eat later at home. A PA system had been set up and so Justin stood up and took the microphone.

"On behalf of my bride and I," he started, and a huge roar of laughter went up from the crowd. "I want to thank you all for coming today and celebrating this important occasion with Lily and I." Then he just sat down again. Justin seemed to run out of words and I thought he was a bit overwhelmed by the occasion, which was unusual for him!

Uncle David then took the microphone. "Friends and *wantoks*. This is a momentous occasion not only for Justin and Lily but also for us as the Moiaimba tribe and people of Mambusu town."

He coughed to clear his throat, probably the result of too much greasy pig fat, and continued.

"The *nenge* bird has revealed itself to both Justin and Lily in recent times and so, in accordance with our culture, we accept them as true leaders of our society. The fact that *nenge* has also, for the first time, chosen a woman for leadership has not escaped our notice. And so we welcome Justin, Lupiano, and Lily not only to marriage but also to a future joint leadership role in our society. There are many challenges ahead but we can be thankful that we now have a husband and wife team to take us into the future."

Once again a huge cheer went up from the assembled visitors. It was very obvious that there was a huge level of support for us from within our community. All of a sudden Justin was on his feet again and taking the microphone.

"I just want to add one comment. Over the past couple of months since I came back to Mambusu, events which have been totally out of my frame of reference or thinking have unfolded. But one thing has been very obvious and that is the support that I and Lily have received from you in my role as Lupiano, headman of the Moiaimba people. It has been overwhelming. Thank you, it gives us great confidence as we step forward now as a husband and wife team in leadership.

"Oh, and one last word. I will be standing for election as the Member for Moi electorate."

To be continued....

POSTCRIPT

The Bird of Paradise that features as the *nenge* bird is a *Lawes Parrotia,* also known as the *six-plumed* or *six-wired Bird of Paradise*. It is one of the beautiful Birds of Paradise found on the island of New Guinea. Video of the bird and its amazing courtship dance can be found on YouTube.

There is no Namel Province and there is no Moiaimba tribe or town of Mambusu in Papua New Guinea. There is no Dept of Social Resources or Member for Moi or Kila Woro. Justin Orlando and his grandfather, as well as Lily and her associates also exist only in the pages of these stories.

If any names in these stories bear a resemblance to any actual persons or place, it is purely coincidental. The words 'moi' and 'nenge' are common in a number of Melanesian languages and their usage here is not representative of any of them. If the use of these or any other word in these stories cause offince, I assure that it is unintentional and offer my apologies.

While the characters in these stories are fictitious, I have tried to maintain historical and soci-cultural accuracy within the stories. I am sure readers, especially those who are familiar with PNG, will identify the characters, places and events as if they were real, while recognising those that in fact, are real.

Please send any feedback to **nengebooks1@gmail.com**.

This story is Book Two in the Nenge Series. Book Three is titled THE PRESENCE OF THE BIRD.

ENDNOTES

1. Statistical information from https://espace.curtin.
edu.au/bitstream/handle/20.500.11937/27064/19060_
downloaded_stream_152.pdf?sequence=2&isAllowed=y
(Curtin University)

Urban Studies, Vol. 38, No. 11, 2017–2036, 2001

Full Circle or Spiralling Out of Control? State Violence
and the Control of Urbanisation in Papua New Guinea.

by Gina Koczberski, George N. Curry and John Connell.